Miseducated

Miseducated

All Learning is Not Academic

JASON WINGERTER

To order additional copies of this book, contact:
Xlibris Corporation
1-888-795-4274
www.Xlibris.com
Orders@Xlibris.com
37565

Dedication

This book would not have been possible without the love, support and encouragement of my future wife and best friend, Ileana. I adore you. For my daughter Madison Paige, whose bright smile and innocence, gives me the inspiration to be all I am capable of being. You are my heart. To Marty Heise, the best supervisor a teacher could have ever had. And to the students of Sayreville War Memorial High School (2001-2004) and their parents for giving me the most wonderful three years of teaching a teacher could hope for.

CHAPTER ONE

" . . . HOURLY OR FOR the night?" the motel clerk asked in an almost unrecognizable Middle Eastern accent.

"How much is hourly?" I inquired.

"Forty-five dollars for four hours", replied the clerk, again barely understanding his response. As I nervously paid for the four hours for the room, I couldn't help but suppress my mixed feelings of both excitement and anxiety. After filling in a fake name and address on the check-in card, I was given the key, as well as directions to my room. As I stood facing the clerk through the bank-teller like window, waiting for him to make me change for my sixty dollars, I distinctly remember the smell of sex in the air. Not the kind you would revisit in past memories and brag to your friends about, but the kind that happens in back alleys or the back seats of cars in the park after dark. The kind you hope no one, especially your friends ever find out about. My immediate thought was that I too would soon smell of this place.

Jarring me from my disturbingly pungent filled day dream, I quickly took the fifteen dollars change and said "Thank you", to the clerk and turned slowly back towards the doors through which I had previously entered. As I approached them, I couldn't help but notice my reflection. Unable to proceed, I just stared back at myself through the reflective – illuminated glass doors. Stopped, dead in my tracks, and unable to move forward, the man behind the counter asked, "Is everything alright, sir?" "Ah . . . yes . . . just fine, thank you . . . I . . . um . . . sorry", and trudged out into the dark abyss of the night, back to the vehicle which had brought me to this den of fornication and lust. Extremely thankful and utterly relieved that I had encountered no other patrons while securing my room, I briskly moved across the uninhabited pavement to where I had parked. Once at my car, I fumbled for the keys and desperately attempted to enter. As I looked down at my hands to find the right key, I noticed how impeccably dressed I was and smirked. As usual, I was dressed to impress. Faded Levi's jeans, camel colored, Italian leather, Bergamo shoes, a white, button down linen Kenneth Cole shirt, untucked, and a suede Tommy Hilfiger sports jacket, colored slightly darker than my shoes. I always dress to impress, I thought. If not for myself, than for those around me. It gives me a sense of security, self-worth, a sort of, . . . fitting in above and beyond the rest, if you will. I looked fantastic and I knew it. Irresistible. However . . . no outfit, no matter how well thought out, could mask my nervousness. I could feel beads of cold sweat, running down the back of my neck, masked by my almost shoulder-length, curly brown hair. In that instant, I felt as if I was a bead of sweat, cold, aimlessly moving along the cologne scented nape of my neck, running for cover, underneath the long, dark curls of night. What was I hiding from? Why was I so nervous? This hadn't been my first sexual tryst with a woman. Hell, I'd even been in places seedier than this. Why was I feeling so apprehensive? Why was this time so different? Was it the location, the time of night? Was it guilt? But guilt about what? Paranoia? Then suddenly it struck me, as clear as my reflection had been minutes earlier in the motel entrance doorway. It was the woman I was to meet. She was the reason for my anxiety and uncertainty. She had a hold over me that no one had ever had before. And this terrified me to the core.

Finally inside my car, I felt slightly at ease, but this sensation lasted only briefly. What was this strange hold over me? Why was I terrified and excited all at the same time? I knew all too well the answer to this question and quickly shook the thought from my mind. After starting the car and backing out of the space in which I originally parked, I gently placed the car in drive and crept forward towards the back of the parking lot, crouched down so as not to be seen or discovered, in search of a remote, unlit area wherein I could hide not only myself, but my car as well, from the world. Moving only at an idled speed, I scanned the other cars in the parking lot, wondering what others were frequenting this establishment on this particular evening. This game, if it were even a game at all, had no social status. Various different types of cars lined the parking spaces in the lot. Two Mercedes, one black one white, a champagne colored Jaguar with Pennsylvania plates, all three expensively beautiful, a beat up old Pinto with replacement-colored front quarter panels, a red t-top Camaro with slightly less than severe front end damage, two SUV's one silver, the other black, both with costly rims and illuminated-installed running boards, three Nissan Maximas from varying years, a blue Toyota pick-up truck that had seen better days, two Hondas, one Civic and one Accord, both green and both of which were aesthetic eye sores, a beautiful Audi TT with tags from Rhode Island, silver and fully loaded, I could only have imagined why in the hell someone from three states up would make the trek to this den of pleasure, three late model mini vans, all from different manufacturers, possessing various stages of use, wear and tear, and a late 90's model Corvette, with its trunk wide open. Nineteen cars in all. All with a different story to tell. One can only assume each one was filled with lies and deceit. What baggage these patrons must carry and what stories their cars could tell. Take the Corvette for example. Its owner must have been in an adamant rush to enter the building, leaving his or her trunk open. And what could they possibly have needed from the trunk? This place wasn't your average sleep over motel. I mean the first question the clerk asked me was whether I needed the room overnight or hourly. And having been here before, I doubted highly if I would see any of the aforementioned cars in the lot upon my departure. Except maybe for the Audi. Ironically, while wondering what story each of these cars could tell about their owners' evening activities, I couldn't help but feel ashamed of them for their deceit as well as their willingness to cast family values aside and risk everything for a few hours of carnal, lustful pleasure. There were three mini vans in the parking lot, and I can only assume that mom and dad, proud owners of said vehicles were not there with the kids, or together for that matter, for an overnight on their way down from the north, heading to Cape May for the family vacation. Especially since children are not permitted anywhere on these premises. But who was I to be so condescending and hypocritical. I mean, I was there for the same reason as probably every other inhabitant of this domicile of sex. What made me so different and better than the rest? What gave me the right to pass judgment and look down upon others in the same situation as myself? Who the hell was I and why was I justifying my actions as acceptable and permitted, unlike everyone else's? What was it? I assuredly convinced myself that it was nothing. Nothing at all. I immediately tried to push the thought from my mind and justify my actions to myself. But it wasn't nothing. It was definitely something. And I was afraid to face it. Afraid to see it. Afraid to acknowledge it. It, was the little difference that set me apart from the dozen or so other individuals here on this particular night, hidden behind closed doors, enraptured in their unbridled appetite for sex and flesh, transported by their expensive foreign cars, over-sized, gas-guzzling road behemoths, family transporters, low income tenements on wheels, and sports cars. What was it that distinguished me from all the rest? Why was I better than any other patron of this motel? Why was I justified in my actions? Love . . .

CHAPTER TWO

THE FIRST TIME I laid eyes on her I almost passed out. She walked into the office of where I worked and I immediately became awestruck. I felt as if I had lost control of all my senses. Everything around me seemed to be moving in slow motion. Never in my life have I seen a woman so aesthetically perfect. It was as if her physical form had been created specifically for me. How could one woman possess such beauty? But there she was, standing not five feet away from me. I was speechless and confused to the point that I was unsure if I was seeing things. Lost. Afraid to move or speak. What was I supposed to say to the woman of my dreams? "Hi, you're perfect."? With as much effort as I could, I picked my jaw up from off of the cold-tiled floor and just about muttered to her in a barely comprehensible tone, "Hey, did you need something?" Her reply, as soft and sweet as it was sexy and alluring, was "Yes, I'm looking for Tom Mathis, the foreign language department supervisor. Laughing internally, not only out of sheer fear of embarrassing myself but also at the thought of Tom arriving at work before nine-thirty, I replied in a firm, yet slightly overly masculine voice, "Do you have an appointment with him?" "Yes", she replied. And there it was. From that moment on, I knew that I had met my one true love, my soul mate, the woman of my dreams. I was even jealous of Tom for having an appointment with her. I wanted her. I needed her. But how could this be? I had spent a mere thirty seconds gawking as well as attempting to talk to this woman and I was ready to give up my days of one night stands and impromptu sexual excursions, bachelor ways and hey days of the single life male? What the hell was I thinking? But as I rounded the desk in the main office and took in her overall beauty from head to toe, I was speechless. She had me, and she had no idea what she had done to me. Never in my life had I felt so out of my own control. How did she get to me? Was she real? Maybe I was just imagining her. I'd seen attractive women before, but never this attractive. Was she out of my league, I wondered, as if that were even possible? The thought of my own self-idolatry, as well as her still lingering beauty humbled me. I was truly at a loss.

In order to save face and not throw myself down at her feet and beg her to love me as I now did her, I replied to her beautifully quipped "yes" in regards to my question about having an appointment and told her that I would check and see if Tom was available. Knowing full well that Tom never arrived this early, I had to keep her around, if only to see her one last time. I calmly proceeded to round the corner of the large, green-marble-topped desk that separated us and pretended to check my mailbox. Herein I was trying to convey to her that her needs were of no such urgency of mine, yet I would get to looking for Tom at my earliest convenience. I wanted to come across as someone of importance. Not just some silly errand boy who attends to beautiful young women, doting on their every need and desire, shirking my own responsibilities and tending to theirs. A good little lap dog I was not. However, this methodical plan of mine was not to be. Upon taking in the full spectrum of this woman's beauty, I instantly forgot what I was doing. Thinking back, I think I may have forgotten who I was for a brief moment. Perfection, as a descriptive term, would not do her justice. Within three feet of her, I carefully, but nonchalantly peripheralized her beauty. She was stunning. My olfactory senses immediately went into high gear and I could detect the scent of expensive perfume and the faint odor of body lotion on her skin. She was dressed all in black, a slimming shade, herein wasted on a figure that needed no such aid. Her hair was long and straight, flowing carelessly down to just above the middle of her back, gently tussled at the shoulder, yet every strand of her shiny black crop was perfectly placed. Her skin was the color of olive green and warm brown sand, the type you imagine seeing at a luxurious, all-inclusive beach resort. Spanish or Italian I immediately assumed, and was to find out later that I was correct in my assessment of the latter. Her nails were long and neatly manicured and painted, as was her make-up and eyebrows. A true vision of utter loveliness. She wore a black camisole top, covered by a black three-quarter sleeve, cashmere sweater wherein only the bottom button was fastened, therein exposing a slightly enticing amount of cleavage given off by her perfectly shaped breasts. The sweater was positioned slightly off her shoulders, allowing the brassiere straps to show through, ever so slightly beneath the straps of her blouse. Upon closer inspection, I could only have imagined how her creamy, soft shoulder felt to the touch. Her lower extremities were covered by an above the knee designer skirt, that hugged her hips and upper legs in a fashion as if it were made specifically for her. From beneath her skirt, her long, toned, tanned legs flowed into a pair of expensive open backed heels, which covered what I could only imagine to be her perfectly pedicured feet. Taking in this view of magnanimous beauty, as it was, only for a second, I instantly forgot about my ploy to act nonchalant and muttered excitedly, "I'll go see if I can find him!"

Scurrying from the office, I found myself covered in sweat. Why was I so nervous? She can't read my mind, I thought. There's no way she could know how I felt about her during our brief encounter. Yet I felt as if she could, and the thought of this terrified me to the core. As I nervously trudged down the hallway, destination unknown, my mind scrambled as to what I would say to her upon my return. Had I acted unsure of myself thus far? I never questioned myself before, but then again I had never been in a situation where a woman or any other person for that matter left me in such a state.

I proceeded down the hall to the other entrance to the office and hurriedly entered the staff bathroom. Once inside, I sat down on the top of the toilet, head in my hands, and took a deep breath. "Come on, you can do this!", I told myself, and immediately stood up and checked my own appearance in the mirror. And there it was. For the first time ever, I was faced with the distinct possibility that someone, a woman in fact, had the power over me to make me feel inferior. But how could this be? I have never before felt so uncomfortable and out of place after meeting someone. Part of me wanted to rush right over to her, profess my love, and convince her to run away with me. Unfortunately, that wasn't an option for me, due to the utter fear and nausea I was at that time currently experiencing. Plus, what would she think of me if I did such a thing? "Less is more", I began to tell myself, "Less is more", and squashed the ridiculous idea from my head. I quickly splashed some tepid tap water onto my face and went forth; ready to tackle the greatest challenge of my life.

CHAPTER THREE

M Y LIFE THUS far had been quite interesting if I do say so myself. I have had various experiences that one would call far from routine and have enjoyed not only the decisions I have made throughout my thirty plus years, but the things I've learned from the consequences of my mistakes. Growing up, I wanted to be a lawyer. A corporate attorney at that. However, once I graduated high school and realized all of the work that would be expected of me, I quickly decided on a career change and chose my major for college. Undecided. Coincidentally it meshed with my views on where my future would lead and in what direction I would take my life. It was a perfect fit. Unfortunately, due to a series of events wherein I chose a college close to home due to the location of my high school sweetheart, I would come to find out that I was more undecided about things than I could have ever imagined. And in choosing my college of choice, with heavy regards to the aforementioned young lady, I was given the major of elementary education by my nameless advisor; apparently a stipulation of playing on a college sports team is that you needed to have a declared major. "Hah", I thought. Why the hell would I ever want to go into teaching? The pay is crap, the students are unappreciative of your efforts, speaking from my own experience as a student and now a teacher for that matter, and as I at the time felt, your colleagues fit into three distinct categories: one, those who truly enjoy the profession and want to make a difference in their students' lives; two, those who were not part of the "in crowd" during their stint in high school and, being that they missed out the first time around, decided to try it as an adult, assuming they would have more clout and feel popular and accepted, meaning they could not function socially around a group of their peers; and three, those who have left other professions assuming teaching to be an easy job with short hours, summers off, doing fun and cutesy projects, being made to feel young by the surrounding youth and having direct power over individuals, even if these individuals are kids. All a bunch of bullshit as far as I was concerned at the time. My attitude was, give me whatever major you want. I'm only here to play ball and get laid. It was not like I was going to actually study, or even attend most of my classes for that matter. I got through my senior year of high school with that attitude and graduated within the top ten percent of my class. Why should things in college be any different? I was one of, if not the big man on campus in high school. People hung out with me, not me with them. I was one of the people you wanted to be seen with. And the girls . . . oh the girls. What college co-ed girl wouldn't want to hook up with an all-American baseball player, who just graduated high school and was up for fun? No responsibility, out at all the big parties or hosting them. No parents around, telling the future leaders of America what to do. Life was grand and I was excited to take it to the next level once I began college.

However, not long after choosing my college of choice and signing a letter of intent to attend and play baseball at the University of New Jersey, my previously mentioned high school sweetheart broke up with me. Two weeks before my high school graduation to be exact. I was heart-broken, devastated, crushed. What was I going to do without her? How could she have been so insensitive to my feelings? I had planned my future education around her physical proximity. Why was this happening to me? I was a good boyfriend. True, I was planning on partying it up in college with a different girl every single night, even though I would still have the same girlfriend. But she left me. That's not supposed to be how things happened. How could she leave me? Especially for some goofy football player named Toby who graduated three years previous? Couldn't he get a girlfriend his own age? Hadn't he been popular his senior year in high school. What happened? What about my feelings?

After about a week and a half of self-loathing and depression, I realized that I was not in love with her, but was upset about how she had made me look. She destroyed my male pride. And as any man will tell you, this is not a comfortable situation to be in. Anyhow, as high school graduation was only a day away and I was able to put my recently broken relationship into perspective, I decided to just let go, in a manner of speaking. I was free, single, sexy, popular, and well-liked, or so I assumed. I didn't need a girlfriend to tie me down. I was going into the adult world a free man, ready to take on the challenges the up and coming summer and pending fall college semester had to offer.

CHAPTER FOUR

F OR SOME STRANGE reason, I've always had trouble recalling the past. I'm not exactly sure why, but my guess is probably that growing up in my family, you needed to lie to survive. Now that is not to say we were completely dysfunctional, stole from one another and were beaten, but our family philosophy deemed it fitting to spare each other's feelings. Unfortunately, no one usually knew who was mad at whom or who was doing what to whom and why. I was the oldest of three boys. Four years separated each birth. Eric was the middle son and Aaron the youngest. Growing up, what memories I have retained and can recall are quite pleasant. My brothers and I were all involved in sports, baseball to be exact, and my parents gave their full attention to making sure we were involved to the extent in which we chose to be. We were lucky. Although my parents were supportive of my brothers and me when it came to baseball, they were never over-bearing, forcing us to do anything we didn't want to do. I should probably have told them how much I appreciated, and still do for that matter, the sacrifices they endured so that my brothers and I were able to enjoy our athletic experiences. Playing sports gave us a basic foundation of following rules, sportsmanship, teamwork, practice, and all those other attributes associated with being on a team and therefore we were able to apply them to the bigger picture, . . . life. Eric was by far the star of the three, making the US National team at 17 and the Olympic team at 19. My father claims that Eric's success was due to my practicing with him while playing baseball in the park with my friends, and never giving him an inch. I just think he had fantastic ability that far superceded mine and fortunately he has been able to parlay those skills into becoming a successful businessman out in the mid-west. Although we see each other infrequently and rarely speak on the phone, I miss him dearly and not a day goes by wherein I don't give him a thought. Eric can be quite difficult at times, opinionated, authoritative, and roughly abrasive and to the point, but he is still my brother and I respect his opinion. Even when it is wrong.

My brother Aaron on the other hand gave up baseball after high school due to a car accident wherein he was hit by a drunk driver and has difficulties with his back to this day. He vaulted himself onto the social scene of college, the first of which I attempted to attend, and after a few years than most, came out with a degree in education. Aaron is a wonderful young man, married, with a son on the way, and I couldn't be more proud of him. Unfortunately, I haven't really relayed that message to him often enough and because of this, there has always been a void in our relationship. I feel partially responsible for this and, even though Aaron can be a pompous ass at times who wants everything done when and how he wants it, I love him dearly. Looking back, I bear the brunt of the blame, due only in fact to the distance in years between us. It was tough enough relating to Eric who was four years younger than I, but with Aaron being eight years younger, I felt we had nothing in common. But he was and always will be my little brother and just recently, I've tried bridging the gap between us, and look forward to advanced success in continuing on this journey well into the future.

My parents attended the same high school, lived only five blocks away from one another, and my father was, for a brief time, my mother's paper boy. Mom, originally from Boston and dad from New York City, both spent their adolescent and teen years growing up in a highly populated immigrant town, made up of mostly of Pollack and Russian, neither of which they were. I've always had a slight affinity for this town and it used to excite me on many levels when we would visit family or when I took my first teaching job in not only the same town, but in the same high school in which my parents attended. My mother's parents were of mostly Irish descent, and my father's Greek and German. What memories I have, up until the time I was eleven, of visiting my grandparents were grand. That is of course depending on which set you were visiting. It's funny what we learn as we grow older and how when looking back at memories we once had, change and take on different forms and shapes when we find out more and more about the past. The more you dig the more you find, even if it is just more dirt. What seems to be on the surface may not always be the case. What I am basically trying to convey, is that things do not always appear as they seem. And what seemed like a nice, quiet little high school in a working-class, blue-collar, immigrant populated town, . . . was anything but. Lies, rumors, deceit, sex, drugs, criminal charges, arrests, bribes, inappropriate sexual misconduct, improperly handled school fund's, theft, adultery, and corruption seemed to surround this tiny athletic driven high school in this tiny little town. And I was beginning my first year of teaching there.

CHAPTER FIVE

ROOM 309. I HURRIEDLY scanned the parking lot for signs of life, rushing through the dark-filled evening air to one of the rear, side entrances of the building. I had made sure to park under the second to last parking lot lamp, for its bulb has been burned out since the first time I'd ever been there. Once inside the stairway entrance, I again noticed the stale smell of sex, a repugnant odor of which I couldn't at the time believe permeated the entire building from front to back, sending my thoughts immediately back to the incident just moments ago wherein I was frozen at the sight of my own reflection in the illuminated doorway. The clerk, jarring my conscience back to reality, was the last thing I needed, and hopefully would be the last person I would see until I entered my room. As I scurried up the stairs, I noticed a peanut M & M wrapper as well as a light blue Trojan condom wrapper. "Huh, sex and a snack.", I chuckled to myself, wondering which condiment went first. And why was it opened here in the stairwell? With that thought breaking through to my conscience, I immediately let go of the banister and carefully watched each step as I ascended the stairs.

At the top of the third floor, still irked by the used wrappers between floors one and two, I reached underneath my shirt and grabbed the door handle, hoping not to find any more surprises. As I turned out into the break of worn discolored carpeting and low lit wall lighting, I could hear nothing. It was as if for only a brief moment, time stood still. Immediately remembering that the management of this establishment had recently installed cameras in the hallways, I steadily but non-chalantly proceeded down the corridor to my room. As I slipped the key into the lock, I briefly pondered how many other sexual encounters had happened in this very room. Using this very key to enter. As soon as the thought entered my mind it was gone, and I entered.

CHAPTER SIX

M Y SENSE OF humor has always been my best defense against my own nervousness. So upon leaving the bathroom, I once again rounded the corner of the large green-marble topped desk and said to the angel I had previously spoken with, "Hey, can I help you?", as if this was our first time meeting. She immediately looked at me dumbfounded and began to stutter. "Didn't I . . . we . . . you just . . . , weren't you . . ." "Just kidding", I replied. Wanting so desperately to relieve her from her brief uncomfortable ness, acting the part of some sort of hero, a knight in shining armor, come to rescue this damsel in distress. And that was when it happened . . . She smiled at me. A smile that left me with a thousand questions, hopes and dreams, and an even greater need to know her, be with her, spend time with her, . . . have her.

Thinking back, it wasn't so much the fact that she smiled at me, but rather how she did it. With a slight flip of her head, she tussled her hair away from her right eye, exposing her perfectly manicured eyebrow, lowered her head gently and tilted it, raising her left brow and lowering her right as if to say something in defense of her initial reaction to my toying with her, and opened her mouth the tiniest bit. Her slightly moist, perfectly full lips gave way to her glowing white teeth. Breathtaking . . . I was in! The initial ice was broken and I hadn't made a complete ass of myself. Wherever our relationship would lead from here excited every living cell in my body. When would I see her again? And why was she meeting Tom of all people? His girlfriend maybe? No, I thought to myself, knowing I would have a better chance with Tom than she. I could only assume she was here for an interview, one in which I hoped with every ounce of my being she excelled.

Still captivated by her smile, I told her that Tom had yet to arrive and it might be a while, due to the fact that he lives in such a far proximity to the school, but that she could wait here in the office and hopefully he would be along shortly thereafter. The confident young woman graciously thanked me and we parted ways. As I walked out into the hallway towards the stairwell to my second floor classroom, I felt as if I had regained my composure and apprehensiveness about being taken so aback by such a beautiful woman. Halfway up the stairs, I was met by one of my students who was beside herself in regards to family problems at home, and as we headed to my room for a session on advice and possible what-to-dos, the woman in black faded from my thoughts as quickly as she had entered.

CHAPTER SEVEN

WHEN INTERVIEWING FOR this job three years previous, I never thought that one place would have such a huge impact on my life. I can remember it like it was yesterday, anxiously awaiting Miss Rachel Hayleigh, language arts supervisor, to arrive and begin my interview for a position as a secondary education English teacher. I was late in applying for this position and had already received three job offers from previous interviews, but had yet to accept any due to varying factors. I assumed the advertisement for this position's vacancy had since been filled, yet was greatly surprised to hear from Miss Hayleigh. Doing quite well thus far in regards to the interviewing process and being just out of college, I felt it a good idea to interview here, even though on the phone Miss Hayleigh sounded as if all the positions had for the most part been filled. I would go, quickly scheduling an appointment for the next day, thinking to myself, if not for another job opportunity, then just for sheer interviewing practice. I at the time liked the idea of possibly teaching in the high school in which my parents both attended and began dating one another, and felt it worthy of my time and effort to apply therein.

The fifty or so minute ride was like traveling through time. Having done this trek numerous times in the past to visit my grandparents, I found the trip to be quite surreal, being that they had since moved from this town many years previous. Surprised at the development along the way as my driver's side window had become a port hole through time, I was flooded with memories of how so many things had changed and was not quite different from my vague recollections of them. Strip malls and shopping centers replaced undisturbed wooded areas. Paved over parking lots and small business buildings with loading docks lined the roads to my destination that were once a forgotten about naturalistic preserve, housing various types of animals. The further along I traveled, the more and more suburban industrialization came into my view. Taking all this in, I felt a bit apprehensive about arriving in my parents' home town, fearful of what it had become. But it wasn't until I hit main street, coming off the bridge that lead into town, that I was truly transported back into time. It was as if nothing had changed. This small little working class town had been able to hold onto its posterity and for the most part, avoid both industrialization as well as real estate development. Aside from a group of low income housing apartments which lined one side of Presidential Park and the new strip mall which lined the other, the rest of this quaint little town had remarkably remained the same. The old baseball field where my father played little league was still in use. The barber shop where my mother's father took me to get my first haircut, to the dismay and disappointment of my father, had changed owners and become a beauty shop, but nonetheless the building still remained and except for the sign in glowing red neon, was virtually unchanged. The 7-11 at the end of Collier Avenue, a place where upon every visit to my grandparents' house, my younger brother Eric and I would walk to buy candy with money given to us by our grandparents, still looked the same. Even the drive-thru dry cleaners and Sully's Funeral Home were still thriving and looked as if they hadn't changed but one bit. Driving through Yarseville was like taking a step back in time. I couldn't believe I was here again after all these years and all at once I was overcome with a feeling of fitting in. After about forty-five minutes, I pulled up to and into the school parking lot. I remembered stories my father had told me about how he would ride his '58 Triumph through the halls of the school during its construction and began picturing my father, jeans and a t-shirt, riding his motorcycle through the halls of the school in which I was about to apply. Immediately, I felt a close bond to not only my father, but to my mother as well, and for the first time throughout my interviewing for teaching positions in different schools, I was excited about the prospect of where it was that I was applying.

CHAPTER EIGHT

ONCE INSIDE ROOM 309, I quickly locked the door behind myself and leaned my back up against it, as if I were hiding from someone or something, securing myself away from this indescribable fear. After a deep sigh of relief from not encountering anyone on my way to the room and being out of the view of the hallway cameras, I carelessly tossed the key and its attached diamond-shaped, green room marker with scratched white lettering onto the top of the television. I was a half an hour early and relieved at the prospect of having a bit of time to myself before Elena arrived. Elena Dimania, I thought to myself as I had done so many times before, was such an exotic name for such an exotic woman. Immediately shaken from the beginnings of my daydreaming, my cell phone rang, therein jarring me back to reality. Upon picking it up and repeatedly saying "Hello", the voice on the other end of the line answered.

"Baby, hi it's me. Just wanted to know if you needed anything before I got there?"

"No, sweetie, I took care of everything. The room number is 309. How far along are you?"

"Just up the road", she replied, saying she would arrive within the next ten minutes.

"Ok angel, see you soon", and I hung up the phone as quickly as I answered it and fumbled for a cigarette. Noticing it was my last, I for a brief moment considered calling her back and asking her to stop and pick me up a pack, but then thought better of it. The thought of her arriving early excited me because it meant more time for us to be together, and I felt as if her early arrival could be translated as she could no longer stay away from me. These suspicions were confirmed upon her arrival via our conversations between love-making. This would be the night I would tell her I loved her.

Many a thought raced through my head during that ten or so minutes I waited for Elena's arrival and I drained every last drag of nicotine from my smoke. While sitting on the edge of the bed, awaiting her arrival, I pondered a bit. What had gotten me to this point? How had one woman been able to put a spell over me so quickly? Where was our relationship going? Up until now I assumed that for her it had just been sexual. Where would it go from here? And why was I so intent on telling her of my love for her. Would this scare her away? How would she react? I had known this woman for less than two months and I was ready to profess my undying love for her and change my ways. How would I . . . "KNOCK . . . KNOCK . . .", interrupted my thoughts, and I quickly moved to the door, opening it and letting in the beauty of a thousand sunsets. She greeted me with a warm embrace, coupled with a moist, succulent kiss, and a whisper in my ear "I'm gonna show you how much I've missed you.", as she led me towards the queen-sized bed.

Looking passionately into my eyes, Elena began running her smooth lips upon my face and neck. I felt as if she were tasting me, smelling me, readying herself for a long overdue meal. As she moved down from my neck to the middle of my chest, she began biting two of the top three buttons off of my shirt and seductively spitting them out, then gently moved her hands down along my hips, stopping only when she reached my belt. Lowering herself down on the floor to where she now knelt before me, she began to unfasten my pants with her left hand while massaging my inner right thigh with her right. Nearing full excitement, not only from the beginnings of her blatant ravaging of my body, I tried to speak when she looked up at me in a coy sort of manner from underneath her shiny dark hair. She pressed her index finger to her lips implying that I should remain quiet, tore open the remaining buttons on my designer shirt and threw me back against the bed. What was to follow afterwards was a carnal exploration of two beings becoming one. That evening we explored every inch of one another's bodies and had had more than our evening's fill of quenched desire. After our third time of lovemaking was complete, I climbed atop of her, pressing my toned, chiseled chest and abdomen deep against hers, gazed deep into her eyes and spoke, "I love you Elena, and I have from the first moment I first laid eyes on you." "I love you too, Jared, and have from the day I met you in the copy room." Thrilled at her retort, I couldn't help but immediately notice that our first encounter had been different for the both of us. How could this have been? Feeling exhilarated as well as confused, I at the time thought better of discussing our conflicting first encounters and instead reveled in the beauty of the moment.

CHAPTER NINE

WHILE WAITING IN the main office, fifteen minutes early for my appointment with Miss Hayleigh, I was greeted by an overly friendly, older woman by the name of Mrs. Martin. She smelled of decade old perfume and was dressed in a manner not reflecting her age, rough around the edges and in dire need of a dye job and make-up. She stood too close, invading my personal space when she spoke, but was friendly nonetheless. Seeing me sitting in the main office in my black Donna Karan suit, olive green Versace' dress shirt, and floral print Uazi tie, she immediately asked if I was interviewing for a position. "Yes", I replied surprisingly, assuming her to be Miss Hayleigh. She then extended her arm, offering up her hand, so as to have me shake hers as if we were in a business meeting, and went on to introducer herself by name, informing me that she was the art teacher here at the high school. Without letting me get in a word edgewise, or letting go of my hand for that matter, she wished me luck. She continued on, telling me how professional I looked, doting on me the way a mother would her son, which, at the time I found to be quite endearing. She then told me to stop by the art room after I was finished, wherein she would give me a yearbook so I could familiarize myself with the faces of other staff members. I thanked her very much and remained seated, patiently waiting for Miss. Hayleigh to arrive, the whole time wondering why she would offer up a yearbook for me to familiarize myself with the faces of staff members when I had yet to even interview for the position. Had she known something I hadn't?

Approximately five minutes before our scheduled appointment time, Miss Hayleigh entered into the main office. She was an older woman in what I assumed at the time was her late forty's, who looked quite good for her age. I immediately noticed her firm, tanned legs growing out from underneath her short blue, linen skirt. Her thighs, and especially her calves, were those of a toned athlete, which I would later find out she was a marathon distance runner. She wore a set of six inch heels that would make a pole dancer envious and before I could complete my once over of this attractive older woman, her short-white haired head spun around to look at me as quickly as she had arrived and said, "You must be Jared Whitmore.", in a more telling tone than that of an asking one. "Miss Hayleigh?" I replied inquisitively, "Pleasure to meet you." As she shook my hand, I noticed what a firm hand shake she had, which was surprising for such a demure older woman. She sincerely apologized for her tardiness which I immediately dismissed as professional courtesy due to the fact that she was in fact early for our appointment, and she asked me to follow her to her office.

As we walked out of the main office, away from the green, marble-topped desk where unbeknownst to me at the time, I was to eventually encounter the love of my life; Miss Hayleigh immediately began to tell me all about Yarseville High School and the language arts department therein. I found her to be professional as well as intelligent, impeccably dressed, and an overall pleasure to speak with. While walking down the long first floor corridor, our backs to what I would later that day learn to be the school's auditorium, we turned right and entered an elevator on our left, situated just across from the guidance offices and right before the entrance to the library. On our walk to the elevator, I briefly told Miss Hayleigh, who had by now told me to call her Rachel, about my affiliation with Yarseville, wherein she stated that she found my past with this small little town as well as this school intriguing. While talking with Rachel, I couldn't help but noticed the enormous size of the school. The walls were painted a drab light blue, lined where the wall's cement ceased showing by tan metal lockers, ranging through an insurmountable variation of numbers. The floors seemed to be old but newly waxed and the emanating smells from the open door classrooms permeated the halls with the scent of old books and chalk dust. As best as I could recall, the scent excited me for some reason, and to this day I'm not sure as to why.

Upon entering Rachel's office, she asked me to be seated in the chair directly inside the door, wherein she pulled up a seat and sat caddy-cornered to me, with the corner of the desk separating us. As she leafed through my portfolio, I began telling her about my education, the three previous colleges I had attended, future plans of study, and my experience in teaching up through this point. I explained to her my background in special education which allowed me to handle a majority of any conceived behavioral issues within the classroom. The conversation, although professional and regarding my application for employment, seemed to flow freely and easily. Rachel seemed to be all about the students' well-being and wanted to hire teachers who in turn wanted the same. This excited me greatly and the longer we spoke, the more comfortable I felt in this environment.

While discussing an instance in which I was physically attacked by one of special education students, there was a knock at the door and we were soon joined by a Mrs.

Janice Brodsky, an archaic-looking English teacher who looked old enough to have taught since the turn of the century. At first glance, I thought this short-haired woman was a man and was relieved that I had waited to greet her until she was introduced to me. Following her apology for being late, Rachel begun verbally singing Janice's praises and conveyed what an asset she was to the Yarseville language arts department. Rachel then asked if I minded if her most valuable employee sit in and participate in the interview. I of course replied "No, not at all", not knowing then what a vindictive, malicious person this Janice would turn out to be.

They began asking me questions about my student teaching experience, likes and dislikes in regards to teaching English, favorite and least favorite subject matter in the realm of language arts, and about lessons I'd created in the past. Finally, they asked me for ideas about certain topics such as poetry, "Romeo and Juliet", expository writing, short stories and novels, questioning me about how I might go about teaching these areas and for possible ideas to keep my students engaged. After about forty minutes or so, Janice excused herself saying, "It was a pleasure to meet you, and good luck." "Thank you very much, nice meeting you as well.", I responded, and after Rachel excused herself for a moment, the two spoke briefly outside in the hallway behind the closed office door.

Before long, Rachel returned, again conveying her utmost confidence in Janice and asked me to follow her just down the hall to a small classroom, wherein I was to be given thirty minutes to write a lesson plan based on Robert Frost's poem, "After Apple Picking". I cannot recall the lesson plan, but only that the computer Rachel had put me on to type the lesson was not working properly. Working under pressure, on what I would later find out was just one of Yarseville's many technological quandaries; I finished the assignment and returned it promptly to Rachel. Once back in her office, I was both delighted and surprised to hear that the position for which she was originally interviewing me for would be given to someone she had already hired. She went on to offer me, on the spot, the job she had since given to the aforementioned someone. Rachel told me that she felt I would be a perfect fit in the position and would just give the recently hired individual, the classes for which I was interviewing.

Ecstatic, I maintained my composure, graciously thanked her for the offer as well as the opportunity, and asked her if I could have a few days to think it over. I told her that I had since been offered three other teaching positions and wanted to give each a bit of consideration. She was more than accommodating and promptly gave me a tour of the school. While on our tour of the facilities, we discussed a variety of things pertaining to the opportunity at hand. Once finished, we shook hands and I thanked her for her time as well as the opportunity and the offer, and assured her that I would come to a decision within the next four days and get back to her as soon as possible. After thanking me as well, Rachel turned on her six inch heels, blue linen skirt, and marathon-toned legs and disappeared around the corner corridor across from the auditorium.

CHAPTER TEN

MY DAYS IN college were difficult to say the least. That is, depending on which institution I'm talking about and which stint of time it is to which I am referring. Shortly after my summer of fun and high school graduation, I was, at least in my own mind, primed and ready to take on the world of college. Still tied to the close to home school I chose in order to be near my high school sweetheart who was now but a vague memory from my past, my plans were to accentuate my life thus far with continued partying and lustful fun. Unfortunately for me, things were not to turn out this way. My first year and a half in college left me with few one night stands, a less than poor grade point average, few friends except for those I associated with on the baseball team, and academic probation. Fed up and completely frustrated by what I would later realize to be my self-induced demise, I dropped out of school and moved to Arizona to live with a buddy of mine from high school. Shortly after realizing this wasn't working out and living with a roommate who had more problems than I, I decided it best to come back to my home town with my tail between my legs, realizing, but never to this day admitting, my parents were right.

For the next eight or so years, I enrolled in the community college close to home, made sporadic classroom appearances, and by the third week of any semester, decided to cut my losses, drop out, and begin again next semester. Working jobs from bartending, to moving furniture, to retail, I eventually came to the realization that I still in fact had no idea what I wanted to do. However, I sure as hell knew what I didn't want to do, and that was to keep repeating the cycle of going nowhere with my life. Somehow or another, I managed to obtain sixty or so college credits via my numerous attempts at obtaining a degree and decided that I would try my hand at substitute teaching. The money was decent, the hours were great, and if I didn't feel like going to work, I could always say I wasn't available. This seemed great! Hell, the last good time I really had was in high school so I figured, why not go back. It would be great. But herein something happened to me. About two weeks into my substituting position at a special education school, I realized something. I was quite fortunate compared to a vast number of individuals in this world and not only did I have the ability and skills to succeed, but teaching gave me the opportunity to give individuals the knowledge, direction, and advice to help others to do so as well. Ironically, I was hypocritically giving advice to others that I myself wouldn't heed. "What a revelation!", I thought. "Finally, a direction in which to move forward. Something that actually excited me." I would register again for school in the fall and take things seriously. My trip back to high school, fortunately for myself, was not like those who become teachers because things didn't go as they planned while attending as students. I was now well on my way to beginning my career in education.

Over the next two years, I reenrolled in my hometown's community college, studied, excelled academically, and received an Associates degree in Humanities. Not only was this experience a breeze, but it was actually fun. Thinking back at the long road in which I had to travel, it seemed at this particular moment, upon my community college graduation, that I had a long and tedious road ahead. But I was motivated, excited, and ready to tackle the next step.

CHAPTER ELEVEN

REPOSITIONING MYSELF ONTO my back, I gently took Elena's head and placed it upon my chest. Looking down at her naked back as I caressed her long black hair, I couldn't help but ask her about her recollection of our first encounter, wondering to myself the entire time I was asking her for her version of our first meeting, how she could have forgotten the incident in the main office. And what the hell is this "meeting" in the copy room. I was perplexed and disappointed at the thought of our first encounter not being of substantial significance to her. How could this be? Who did she think that was that so coy fully played with her while she waited for Tom? Afraid to hear, but needing desperately to know, I asked her about her version of our first encounter and proceeded to listen to her tale.

"It was a Wednesday morning, second period", she began, "and I was sitting in the downstairs teacher's lounge looking at the abundance of paperwork I'd since received upon beginning this job just two weeks prior." "I had spent all my second periods there, not really knowing anyone or having anywhere else to go for that matter."

Sitting up abruptly in bed and throwing back her hair as well as her right leg over my left, straddling my naked body, she looked down at me with excitement and determination to tell the story as seen in her eyes, and she proceeded to speak.

"I was looking at my class lists, still trying to make some semblance of it all when I heard your voice. You had moments ago come in to the room without my knowledge and began making copies. Hearing your voice, I felt compelled to turn and see who it was and there you were. I had seen you once before but only from a distance. I thought you were attractive then, but this up close and personal, you were more than I had imagined."

"Get outta here!", I said as I tried to grab her wrists and toss her soft, subtle body off mine. "You're making this shit up."

"Sssh, let me finish.", she replied.

"Trying to take you all in in an instance was overloading my senses. I immediately felt the need to know you, be with you, have you. I abruptly stood up, turned, extended my hand, and introduced myself."

"Don't you remember any of this?", interrupting herself.

"Of course I do baby, I just . . . (thinking better of sidetracking her story and correcting her as to the first time we met, I quickly agreed and let her finish her version) . . . want to hear it from your perspective my love."

"Then let me finish.", she quipped.

"In taking your hand in mine, I couldn't help but gaze deeply into your ocean blue eyes. I needed to touch you, somehow, in some way, if only for a brief moment. I needed to experience closeness to you. At that moment I wanted to be the center of your universe. Unsure of what to say next, I nervously turned and sat down; still reeling from our first touch."

"Wow", was at the time all I could come up with, trying to sound sincere but at the same time bewildered at who it was she thought greeted her in the office the day of her interview. Touched by her story as well as the thought that someone so beautiful as she could find me so attractive, I gazed deep into her chocolate brown eyes, moved her ever so carefully from atop my body, laid her on her back and slowly climbed upon her. "That was beautiful honey. I love you."

"I love you too, baby", she replied, and I proceeded to press myself deep into her, still wondering who it was she thought she met that day in the office.

CHAPTER TWELVE

O NCE RACHEL HAYLEIGH rounded the corner and was out of sight, I quickly recalled the art teacher, Mrs. Martin, and her offer to show me one of the yearbooks. Seriously considering taking this position and fresh off of my tour of the school, I was confident I would be able to find the art room, Mrs. Martin, and the book containing the cast of characters that would forever change my views on education. To my surprise, I was able to quite easily find Mrs. Martin's room. Seeing her through the window, I notice a balding portly gentleman who had a perpetual grin on his face. A sort of an eerie look for someone to constantly have, I thought at the time, but had no idea at the moment of introduction, how much eerier it would become. Waiting a moment, to see if I was interrupting, I slowly entered the room and excused myself.

"Mrs. Martin?", I said, in an inquisitive like tone.

"Jared, hi. Call me Doris. I'm so glad you remembered to come by." This is Gary." Gary Pontier. One of the most disturbing individuals I would ever come to meet. On the surface he seemed very friendly. He happily shook my hand, told me that he was an English teacher there at the school, and went on to say that he was the self-proclaimed social director of fun teachers' events. Upon completion of his self pontification, he told Mrs. Martin he would be back in a bit, shook my hand again, and said that he'd hope to see me this up and coming school year.

Once Gary left, I turned to mention the yearbook to Mrs. Martin, and she was already flipping through the pages of it on her desk. She searched desperately for the staff section of photographs, cursing the hard-back, dark-blue encased book with silver lettering on the cover, as if it was working against her to hide her sought after section.

Upon finding it, she gave out a small "Ah, here we are!", and motioned for me to come around her taller than normal desk and join her so as to better see the pictures at hand. Rounding her desk, I noticed what utter disarray was laid out before me. It was as if a bomb had gone off and no one ever cleaned up the mess. "Well, to each his own", I thought and began listening to her tell me about my future co-workers.

After spending about ten minutes or so looking at pictures of staff members from last year's yearbook, I couldn't help but be taken aback by her attitude in that what she was basically doing was giving me her opinion as to who to trust and who not to. "Was this happening?", I said to myself at the time. "Who in their right mind does such a thing?", I thought. Once she was finished giving me her opinion on every photographed staff member within the pages of this book, I thanked her for being so hospitable and she then gave me the book as a gift. Graciously I accepted, if only to show the book to my parents as a sort of memento from a time long since past and made my way back out into the parking lot, pondering my possible future at Yarseville High School.

CHAPTER THIRTEEN

AFTER JUST TWO days of deliberation, I finally came to a decision and quickly called Miss Hayfield on her cell phone to inform her I would be accepting her offer. Picking up the phone on the first ring, she began laughing and told me that for some strange reason, she had a feeling it was me on the other end of the line and asked me if I had made my decision. I proceeded to thank her for the opportunity and told her that I would be accepting her offer. Excited as she was, she asked if there was a possibility for me to come in today and meet one of the vice principals. Why not, I figured, might as well get the ball rolling at full speed, and informed her it wouldn't be a problem. She said we could set up the interview with vice principal, Sarah Innocenzi for two o'clock, and then following that I could go over to the board office to meet Mr. Thistle, district superintendent. "Great I said. See you at two.", and hung up the phone, excited at the decision I had made.

Getting ready to go anywhere was all dependent on my own mood. Of course I would always dress for the occasion; however, I had to feel right in my attire, regardless of what anyone else thought. Upon hanging up with Miss Hayfield, I quickly jumped in the shower, washed and then moisturized myself with baby oil, and then rinsed. Patting myself down with a towel, I tucked my long curly brown hair behind my ears and opened up the medicine chest, therein retrieving my razor, before shave oil, after shave cream, and shaving gel. The combination of these three products, a combination which has taken me about fifteen years to have perfected, seem to work perfectly with my skin's sensitivity and texture. Once finished the painstakingly long and arduous regiment of shaving, I began staring at myself in the mirror. Not saying anything aloud, I remember mentally asking myself, "Why am I interviewing with the vice principal if I was already offered the job?" Chuckling to myself, I quickly chalked it up as just a formality and began my next stage of preparedness.

My hair, although naturally curly, tends to at times have a mind of its own. Although it never looks the same twice, I desperately work to keep it in the same genre so as I am comfortable with its look. On this day however, meeting the vice principal and superintendent, I would have to tone it down a bit. Get rid of some of the rock star volume, taming it tighter and closer to my head, therein giving the appearance that it was not as long as it truly was. There are two types of product I use in my hair, and today, being that the two up and coming meetings could very well have a large impact on my future, I decided to use hair clay as opposed to hair glue. Drying on its own, my crop gives off the illusion of me being a mad scientist. Therefore, it takes a lot of hard work and effort to give me that natural, in/out of control, look. My hair, even more so than my clothes, must be perfect, at least in my eyes. This process could at times take up to an hour in trying to get it just right. Today however, I was lucky. Fifteen minutes later, and I was already in my bedroom, choosing the day's outfit.

I felt it very important to look stylish as well as professional. One of the first things I noticed about Rachel, my new supervisor-to-be, was how impeccably dressed she was. Someone who placed that much time and effort into dressing herself would surely notice the dress of others. "Not a problem for me", I immediately thought, knowing that I as well put a lot of effort into my appearance. I entered my closet and gazed into the long full length mirror and myself. Nonchalantly, I unfolded the white bath towel from around my waist and stood gazing at myself, wearing only what God gave me. Thinking of what to wear so as to make a good impression at the day's interviews, I remember while gazing at my naked body, that I wished I had bigger bones and was about four inches taller. That having been the case, I would have felt perfect within my own skin and would probably never again be self-conscious.

I began right away searching for my tan Perry Ellis slacks, no pleats or cuffs, and slid them on over my baby-oiled legs and backside. Reaching up, I took from off of its hanger, a sky blue Christian Dior dress shirt and slid it over my tanned, toned back. While buttoning up the shirt, I slid into a pair of black leather Herrachi Italian shoes and upon tucking in my shirt, put on and fastened my Melani belt of the same color and material. Before exiting the closet and making my way down to the car, I grabbed my abstract-designed blue, black, and peach Erus tie and my black Versace' sports jacket and hurriedly moved down the stairs, grabbing my keys, wallet, cell phone, and smokes. Briefly catching a glimpse of myself as I turned to lock the door behind me, I couldn't help but smile, laughing at myself for what a vain son-of-a bitch I had become.

CHAPTER FOURTEEN

COMING OFF OF a noteworthy two years in community college, wherein I graduated with honors, I felt undeserving to take the time to step back and revel in the accolades of my accomplishments. I was on the fast track to success, and a small, two-year associates degree from a community college at twenty-six years old was nothing to brag about. So, I immediately began applying to four year schools, ready to move forward and take on the next step of my plan. My first idea was to reenroll in the college in which I first attended and dropped out while on academic probation. My thought process was that they would see my grades from the community college, see what a wonderful turn around I had made, and want to be a participant on my road to success. Also, my mother worked there so I assumed getting accepted, even via my nepotistic advantage, would be a no-brainer.

After interviewing with an admissions officer and explaining that my first attempt here at college almost ten years previous, was doomed to fail for a number of predicating factors, the most important being that I was just not ready for college; and my attendance was more so, if not all, my parents idea of what they felt I should do without really consulting me. Neither of them had received a college education and of course, always wanting more for your children than you have for yourself is very important, they therein pushed me to get an advanced education in order to better my future. I unfortunately wasn't seeing things as they were at the time and explained to the admissions officer that this was the reason for my sitting here in this position before her today.

Seemingly moved by my story, the young lady seemed quite impressed by my accomplishments I had since been able to make but told me in a tone resembling not disappointment or disdain, but in an, oh well sort of manner, that if I wanted to return to this ridiculously pretentious university, I would have to do so whilst remaining on academic probation for the next year and a half. This meant that I would only be allowed to take two classes per semester, had to maintain a B- or better grade point average in both of my classes each semester, and had to register as a non-matriculated student. Code for I could sign up for whatever crappy classes are left after each and every class of students sign up for theirs. Crushed at the thought of this process taking me ten years or so just to receive a Bachelor's Degree, I thanked the woman for her time and informed her that I was no longer considering attending this educational institution.

On my walk back to the car, I remember feeling nothing but defeat. What was I going to do now? I had a plan and this set back was not a part of it. How could this be? Frustrated, I began telling people about my predicament where I was working as a special education teacher's assistant. I had by this time been hired full time and thoroughly enjoying the experience, therein verifying even more so how much I wanted to become a teacher, when about a week later, one of the women I worked with told me about an all-girls Catholic college that was co-ed in the evenings. She said that she had earned her undergraduate degree there and that it was a wonderful experience. Immediately excited about the prospect of my plan still being feasible, I shortly thereafter made an appointment with one of the admissions officers and was again ready to sell myself.

CHAPTER FIFTEEN

T HE TIME HAD finally come and I could no longer wait to ask. Exhausted and covered in sweat, I pulled the covers up to both our waists and propped myself up onto my left elbow, gazed into her eyes as she lay motionless on her back, noticing that she too was out of breath, but maintained a rosy glow about her cheeks that I knew I would not soon forget, and asked;

"Elena?"

"Yes, Jared?"

"Do you remember the day you came into Yarseville looking for Tom, and you met that guy in the office who told you that he would go and look for him?"

"Yeah, sort of. What about him?"

"That was me!" I exclaimed. "Who the hell did you think you were talking to?"

"That was you?" she replied shockingly. "I thought you were the janitor." The janitor, I thought. What the hell was that supposed to mean? How could someone meet a person on two different occasions, one time thinking they were the janitor and not paying them an ounce of attention, and the next time falling hopelessly in love? We had a connection. She found me witty and exciting. I engaged her with my charming ways.

"As a matter of fact, when that guy left the office and came back in, asking me again if I needed any help, I thought he was a little strange. Are you sure that was you?" she replied. Dumbfounded, I just sat on the edge of the bed gazing forward. It just didn't make sense. Then all at once, it hit me.

Still in a state of utter shock in regards to how Elena viewed me as some psychologically challenged custodian, I began to defend myself, as if I was hanging on to something for dear life. She was not going to forget about my . . . our first true encounter, and whether or not she wanted to believe it to be the case, I would have to defend myself as to why she hadn't remembered me.

For the first time since revisiting this long played out movie in my head of our first encounter, I was able to remember what it was that I was wearing. And it was not a pretty recollection. "Yes!" I thought to myself. Now it all makes sense. It was my first day back after being out for a day and half plus the weekend with pneumonia. Bronchial to be exact. I remember feeling lousy that Monday morning of our initial meeting, considering much earlier staying home another day. Knowing what a nightmare being absent can be, and trying to have my students catch up on my lesson plans, I decided to press on and show up at school. Hell, I'd only missed Thursday afternoon prior, being that we had a snow day on Friday.

Point being, I still felt lousy. And because of this, I, on this rare occasion, did not put much time and effort into either my outfit or my hair and overall appearance. I was ill and could have honestly cared less who knew about it. Unfortunately for me, it happened to be on the day I met an angel.

At first conveyance of this story to Elena, she thought I was making it up and told me that there was no way that it was me that day in the office. I repeatedly assured her, explaining the entire morning down to every last word each of us had spoken as well as the exact outfit she was wearing. Half embarrassed, she stood before me, her naked body silhouetted in the bathroom light. She took a cigarette pack from within her brown leather Fendi purse, shook one out of the end of the pack, effortlessly placed it between her perpetually, moistened full lips and lit the end. After taking two drags followed by exhales of blue, plume-clouded smoke, she knelt down beside me, stroked my left cheek with her right hand, and told me she adored me. This, as she would later explain to me, was a greater feeling than love.

CHAPTER SIXTEEN

O N THE DRIVE over to Yarseville for my two o'clock interview with vice principal, Sarah Innocenzi, I could barely subdue my excitement. Primed, ready, confident, and dressed to impress, I would sell myself to Mrs. Innocenzi as I did to Miss Hayleigh and the job would be mine. Smoking more than usual for the majority of the drive there, I decided to take the long scenic route, making an attempt at being able to fully relax before my appointment.

Arriving twenty minutes early for my interview, I pulled into a numbered parking space on the west end of the building. Smoking my last cigarette before entering the building, I noticed a familiar face of someone I had met before. It was Gary Pontier, Yarseville English teacher, and future department colleague. He was leaving the building with a small cardboard box tucked under his left arm and seemed to be in sort of a nervous rush. Not thinking anything of it at the time, I continued to watch Gary in my rearview mirror as the trunk of his late model Mercury Cougar opened and he placed the aforementioned box inside. After a moment or two of what seemed to be his rearranging of items, he quickly glanced around from over his open trunk as if to see if he was being watched, then closed it and made his way back into the building. Even though I noticed him and he had not noticed me, I at the time thought better of drawing my presence to his attention and say hello. Not only because I now had an interview within the next ten minutes, but I also didn't want to awkwardly become engaged in a conversation with someone I for some reason didn't trust from the moment I met. I couldn't place my finger on it at the time, but I knew it was something. And what I would eventually come to find out, should have blown the lid off of this tiny little town and rocked the community to the core.

Making sure I was promptly on time for my appointment, I entered the main office with five minutes to spare, and carelessly tossed the stick of gum into the trash can outside the main office doors which I had been chewing to mask the smell of cigarettes. Just as soon as I sat down, Miss Hayleigh entered the office and greeted me with a smile from ear to ear and a firm handshake, saying "I'm so glad you're going to be with us. I have a feeling you're going to fit in perfectly." She then motioned for me to follow her around the corner, in front of where the secretaries sat, and led me to vice principal Innocenzi's office door.

Upon noticing the two of us standing at her door, Mrs. Innocenzi began motioning for us both to enter with a wafting wave of her hand, pointed to the two chairs in front of us from behind her desk and directed us to sit. She was on the phone, desperately trying to discontinue the conversation and begin our interview. It was then that I realized what an annoyingly nasal-sounding voice she possessed. Once off of the phone, she graciously apologized, smiled and extended her arm, giving forth her hand. Being the gentleman that I am, I immediately stood, extended my hand in return, and thanked her for seeing me. Miss Hayleigh began the conversation by telling Mrs. Innocenzi about my educational background and past work experience in education.

Watching Mrs. Innocenzi throughout the interview, I couldn't help but notice how disorganized and haphazard her thought processes were. While asking me questions, one in particular, I found her attempts at asking me these questions to be both juvenile and benign. "How could a woman holding such a position of educational authority be such a flake?" I thought. Desperately trying to figure out what she was trying to ask of me for the brief fifteen minute interview, my patience were rapidly wearing thin and I began desperately making attempts to rephrase her questions. I later realized that what she was trying to do was to illicit a certain response from me, via asking me questions in a manner in which she was hoping for an appropriate response. "Was this interview even necessary?" I wondered to myself. How could Miss Hayleigh be so professional, polished, intelligent, and exude the aura of a professional educator, while across from me sat an ex-twenty plus year math teacher who was as disorganized as she was unknowledgeable about her job, conversationally challenged, fashionably impaired, and just an overall nightmare to interview with in general. Handbook Heddy, as I would eventually come to call her for her utter lack of knowledge about the rules and regulations of the school. She was so unknowledgeable that she carried around the school's handbook with her wherever she went, desperately leafing through its pages for an answer to any question asked of her. We painfully finished our interview after a brief amount of time and, standing up from my chair, she welcomed me to the family there at Yarseville. I once again thanked her, shook her hand, and exited, wondering the whole time how such an inept individual could be in charge of certain aspects of young children's' lives. Unimpressed and somewhat embarrassed at her lack of professionalism, I left for my meeting with the superintendent, assuming incorrectly that things could not get any worse.

CHAPTER SEVENTEEN

S ETTING UP AN appointment with Ms. Baker was as nerve-racking as it was exciting and the drive to Lakeburne left me with a nervous twinge in the pit of my stomach. "This was it." I thought. "My last chance at receiving an education at an institution to obtain a degree in the field I truly wanted to pursue. What if the admissions officer had the same attitude as the admissions officer from the school I previously attended and tried to return to?" I didn't have it in me to again experience the disappointment of not being admitted into a four-year school, therein leaving me no other alternative but to either change careers, or work on my bachelor's for the next ten years. The thought of this possibility nauseated me. I could feel the sweat coursing down the back of my neck as I exited the highway, just minutes away from facing my future educational fate. Once off the interstate, I merged onto the main route in town and was just fifteen or so blocks away. It felt as if time had stopped and I was moving in slow motion. "Stop being so nervous", I continued telling myself. Pulling over into a strip mall parking lot, I abruptly pulled into a space at the deserted back end of the lot, flung open the door, quickly tucked my tie into my shirt, and vomited all over the aged black pavement.

Regaining my composure after just a brief few minutes, I again was on the road and rapidly approached my future. Driving through the gates past the security booth, wherein I was given directions to my appointment destination by a uniformed, overly serious but very friendly security guard, I idled down the windy road, parking beneath a sycamore tree that grew up from beneath the boundaries of the far corner of the parking lot. Grabbing nothing but a pen, a pad, and a copy of my previous colleges' transcripts, I headed into the language arts building, determined to accomplish what I had set out to do.

Once inside the building, I was immediately greeted by Ms. Baker. She was an average looking, middle-aged woman, late thirties early forties I at the time assessed, small in stature in accordance to height, and thin framed. She wore wire-rimmed glasses that hid her innocent hazel colored eyes, giving off the impression that she was younger than her years would tell. She was dressed quite conservatively, and bore not a stitch of make-up. Her skin was soft yet frail, wherein when she introduced herself to me in what I would describe as a meek, high-pitched voice; I shook her hand and feared breaking it if I had applied any pressure at all.

"What a pleasure it is to meet you, Mr. Whitmore." She emphatically stated, and proceeded to lead me to our meeting area. She had a sweet, caring sense about her while listening to my situation and I at the time truly believed that she could feel my anxiety about the future.

"It has been ten years since I first began college right out of high school and I am a different person now. I have goals and dreams I want to fulfill and am excited about my future possibilities. I know I have made mistakes in the past, but have learned from them. I have to be honest and tell you that I don't regret any of them. Now I know that may sound strange, being that these past decisions have left me with the consequences in which I have to deal with here today, however, those decisions and their consequences have made me who I am. Maybe I've left myself no other choice but to do things the hard way, but I'm doing them my way, and I truly feel that that will make all the difference."

Looking down at my hands upon completing my verbal bearing of my soul, I nervously awaited Ms. Baker's response. Pausing a few moments before speaking, she reached out her hand, gently attaching herself to my wrist, lowered her head to a level beneath mine, therein forcing me to notice she was trying to have me make eye contact, and said in a reassuring, motherly voice, "Let's see how we can make you a member of this institution."

CHAPTER EIGHTEEN

L EAVING MRS. INNOCENZI'S office, I felt relieved as well as confused. Relieved that such a ridiculous formality was complete, and confused as to how this woman landed a job in administrative education, or even as a teacher for that matter. Desperately trying to clear my mind of the experience, Miss Hayleigh interrupted my thoughts as we walked down the hallway corridor adjacent to the main office, "Do you know how to get to the administrative offices at Simler Elementary School from here?" Jarring my conscience back to the present and reminding me that my meeting of administrative members was only half finished, I quickly replied, "No, I'm not sure." While getting directions from Rachel, I couldn't help but feel excited about my next meeting. Barely comprehending what it was she was saying, I again asked her to repeat the directions, sloppily jotted down the names of streets and where to turn using abbreviations, and repeated them back to her. "Perfect!" she said and asked me if I could call her here at the office upon finishing my meeting with Superintendent Thistle. "No problem at all." I said and made my way out into the hot afternoon sun, taking off my sports coat and tossing it over my right shoulder, As I began the walk to my car, I felt myself moving along the whole distance to and through the parking lot with an air of utter assuredness.

Driving over to Simler Elementary School, I drove through town, taking in its entire splendor, eagerly anticipating the up and coming year in which I would be educating the young minds of children from within the hallowed walls of the school in which my parents once attended. I could only imagine how proud of me they, my parents, would be upon hearing the news of my recently acquired teaching position here in Yarseville, their old home town.

Once parked, I snugly fastened my tie up between my shirt collars and effortlessly threw on my sports jacket. Walking across the parking lot towards the smaller than I had imagined elementary school on Kennedy Boulevard, I couldn't help but notice the bright yellow, new model Corvette parked in the space nearest the doors. Upon closer inspection, I noticed the white, block lettering etched into the asphalt in spray paint at the open end of the space, barely peering out from beneath the rear end of this loud colored, high performance sports car. Superintendent. "How odd" my initial reaction was to why a superintendent of a school district would drive such a flashy car, but proceeded nonetheless towards his office, shaking the inference from my head. Inside the doors, I peered my head into a large open office on the right which housed two elderly women hustling and bustling amongst a mountain of paperwork and perpetual phone calls, excused myself, and asked if someone could tell me where to find the superintendents office. "Straight behind you, second door on the right.", the woman closest to me pleasantly stated, and after thanking her, turned and made my way to meet with Superintendent Thistle.

The wait outside of his office seemed an eternity and I remember being torn between thinking it was normal that it was taking so long because my appointment time was not solidified in stone, rather only based on whenever I was finished with my interview with Mrs. Innocenzi. The other being that along with the whole motif of pomposity, previously brought to my attention by the car this man drives, I thought maybe he was just exuding his power and position to inconvenience me and make me wait. Hoping it was the latter, I would soon find out how very wrong I was.

CHAPTER NINETEEN

T WO WEEKS HAD passed since I met with Ms. Baker, and I was anxiously awaiting word from her as to my acceptance to her affiliated college. It was a Thursday afternoon and I was home from work around the usual time, when there in the mailbox, strewn haphazardly amongst two bills, the weekend finder (a small newspaper about the goings on around town), and a zero percent finance credit card application, was the answer to my future. I was holding the direction to which my life would take me, right there in my hands. Standing and looking at the envelope for what felt like an eternity, I turned and made my way back into my apartment and locked the door behind me. I for some reason felt the need to be secure, by myself, ready to face and deal with whatever decision lie within envelope. Dropping the rest of the mail onto the table, I tossed the letter onto the couch and proceeded into the bathroom. Once there, I took a long hard look at myself in the mirror, splashed some water onto my face, patted the dampness off with a towel, and told myself that no matter what that letter said, everything would be alright.

Sitting down on the couch, beer in hand and cigarette dangling from out of the corner of my mouth, I carefully and cautiously inspected the letter. Placing my beer on the table and the cigarette in the ashtray, I picked up the enveloped and held it with both hands. Nervously, I fidgeted, wondering whether or not its lack of girth was a good or bad sign. Not being able to stand the suspense any longer, I tore into it, ready to accept my fate.

CHAPTER TWENTY

PATIENTLY SEATED IN the large oversized administrative office room, one of the secretaries from behind the large L-shaped counter rose from behind her desk and motioned for me to follow her. Confident, but not cocky, I diligently followed the secretary into Superintendent Thistle's office. I had yet to conjure up any ideas in my mind as to what he might look like, however, the moment I entered his office and saw him, I instantly felt his appearance to be fitting. "Mr. Whitmore." he beckoned in a boisterous, lower than normal voice, and without extending his hand for me to shake, leaned back in his overly expensive Italian leather office chair, and placed his faux leather cowboy boots a top his ornate mahogany desk, resting his head in his hands as he cupped them both, interlocked his fingers, and placed them behind.

At first glance, I was able to surmise him to be a tall, stocky man with salt and peppered, thinning hair and matching beard. I couldn't help but immediately wonder whether he kept a beard to hide his larger than normal jowls which were easily visible, even through his unevenly groomed beard. Heavily aged, especially around the eyes, his face was wrinkled and weathered. His eyebrows were solid black in color, though in dire need of trimming. The expression on his face was one of condescension and disgust, both of which remained in tact for the duration of our meeting. He was older, probably well into his fifty's, yet had an attitude as if he was a virile twenty-one year old with the body of an athlete and a twenty-four hour erection. At least thirty plus pounds overweight, I immediately thought of how he would have handled falling backwards out of the chair, therein landing flat on his ass. His dress was just as bad, if not worse than his personal grooming. Along with his faux leather cowboy boots, he was wearing a pair of blue corduroy pants that, upon later inspection when he stood and paced the room, treating me as if I were a captured animal within his lair, were about three inches too short. His shirt was abstractly horrific; its details have permanently been erased from my memory. His tie was nearly as unfitting as his oversized Harley Davidson belt buckle and fashioned in a manner wherein it rose four inches above his waist. I couldn't believe that someone so aesthetically challenged could possess such a position of power and prestige.

Standing there in front of him, I was not only appalled at his ignorance in ignoring my extended hand in which to shake, but his allowance of me to stand without offering me a seat as he lounged behind his desk like a beached walrus, warming himself in the glow of the morning sun. He began our conversation telling me that Miss Hayleigh seemed quite impressed with me; however, he would have the final say on the matter of whether or not I would be hired. "What a prick!" I thought. "What crawled up his ass and died? This jerk off won't even offer me a seat and he's already telling me that if he doesn't like me, I'm out on my ass."

Fired up by his lack of respect and overblown self-image, I was about to tell this self-righteous, ridiculously dressed grandfather to go fuck himself, but quickly assumed that my interactions with him would most probably be minimal and I thought better of blowing my lid and act as foolish as he. I would deal with his condescension and attitude, if only to not reduce myself to his level and secure a position within the district I so desperately wanted to work.

He began our meeting in a most peculiar way. Still standing, he asked me if I knew the name of so and so's cousin from some Shakespearian play, both names of which now escape me. Having no idea of the answer as well as wondering why the hell he was even asking me this question, my only alternative was to respond with, "No sir, I've no idea what his name is." Jumping to his feet as if to be first in line for the all you can eat buffet, he sauntered around his desk, lowered himself to my eye level while crossing his arms in front of himself, and spoke with a scented breath of onions and eggs. "Thistle." he said as if to tell me that the character was named after him. Not knowing what to think about this strange topic of conversation, my only response to his inept social skills as well as his boasting about his being connected to a Shakespearian play was, "Wow, . . . neat. I never knew that." And why the hell should I have for that matter. Wasn't the point of me being here to meet the superintendent and talk salary and education? I didn't know I was going to have a pop quiz on asinine trivia by a bloated, over-confident, self-proclaimed know-it-all who felt his shit didn't stink. If I had, I'd have worn my jerk off repellant.

Shortly after he finished his brazen strut around the room, he asked me the usual questions of why I wanted to work in His district, what I could bring to His high school, and the like. Cautiously answering each and every question in a manner so as to have him believe that he was omnipotent and I was ever so grateful for his offering me this position, we finished up in about twenty minutes, him wishing me luck and me thanking him for the opportunity and I left, relieved and hoping to never have to see this man again. And I never did sit down.

CHAPTER TWENTY ONE

"I WOULD LIKE to extend to you, Mr. Jared Whtimore, my most sincere congratulations and inform you that you are hereby officially accepted to Long Branch College . . .", was as far as I could read when my arm holding my acceptance letter and virtual open door to my educational future went limp, falling aimlessly into my lap. I had done it! All the hard work and effort I put into turning my life around and making something out of myself would soon become a reality. Sitting there, basking in the glow of my own hard work and success, I couldn't help but be proud of myself. Nothing could stop me now. I was on my way to bigger and better endeavors. Primed, excited, and ready to move forward, I anxiously awaited the fall semester to begin, therein affording me the opportunity to become one step closer to my goal as a licensed educator.

Finishing the last swallow of beer from within the bottle and making sure the cigarette in the ashtray, long since forgotten was out, I decided to celebrate my future opportunity, and took a long restful, well overdue nap.

CHAPTER TWENTY TWO

THE FALL SEMESTER began on a hotter than usual, late August afternoon and I had purposely arrived early, so as to not be late for my first class. It was about an hour before its start and I thought it a good idea to walk around campus and familiarize myself with the surroundings. Having been here only twice before, initially to meet with Ms. Baker in regards to admittance, and just two months prior, registering for my classes and buying my books, wherein, I was in a rush and was not at the time able to stay and look around, I found the grounds to be beautiful as well as peaceful. "Strange how quiet things look.", I thought to myself after passing and waving to the security guard, pointing to the affixed parking decal in my rear-left passenger window, allowing me access to the school's grounds. Once parked, I gathered my materials, threw them into my bag, lit a cigarette, and made my way out into the academic world wherein I would spend my next two years.

The walk to Hillary Hall, where I would eventually come to find out would house most of my classes, was a brief one, connecting directly to the parking lot where I'd parked. There were numerous parking spaces available, which at first surprised me, then remembered that Long Beach College was an all-girls Catholic school that was co-ed at night. Members of the male gender were only permitted to take classes after four P.M. and assumed upon my arrival, the campus would consist of only slightly less than middle aged men, returning to college at a later in life period in time. The campus itself, was ironically set in a small little Orthodox Jewish community, wherein driving through town to school every day was like taking your life into your hands. Kids were running around aimlessly without being supervised, drivers not looking where they were going, everyone acting as if they had the right of way, and to make matters worse, they all dressed the same, making it at times difficult to tell them apart. I remember one instance when an elderly gentleman walked right out in front of me between two cars and never even acknowledged my presence or thanked me for not running him over. Then, just two blocks further and thirty seconds later, the same man, or so I thought at the time, pulled out from a parking space and cut me off, acting as if he had the right of way and I had no business on that street to begin with. All in all, it was a strange mix of communities.

Stopping just outside the main entrance doors to Hillary Hall, I sat down on the steps leading in and proceeded to take the last three drags of my smoke. Taking my bag from off of my shoulder and placing it on the bottom step at my feet; I began to notice something very peculiar I had not picked up on during my two previous trips here. There were girls everywhere. Different sizes, shapes, heights, colors . . . you name it, this place had it. The end of summer was but a brief memory and scantily clad young women carpeted the campus. Short skirts and shorts, tank tops, and sandals adorned the majority of the school's students. Girls were lying out, sunning their toned young bodies in the late afternoon sun. Small study groups of three or four young women, casually lounging around barefoot in the grass, discussing topics ranging from philosophy to art, accentuated the landscape. Different types of women, away from home, inexperienced, perceivably easily coerced, and ripe for the picking. Unfortunately, I was about ten years too late for this virtual cornucopia of college girl "fun" and was determined to remain focused on my studies. But at a ratio of 38:1, women to men, staying focused on my studies wasn't going to be easy. Realizing the time, I quickly jumped up from my voyeuristic position on the stairs, grabbed my bag, flew through the two glass sets of double doors that gave admittance to the building, and hurriedly ran up the stairs to the room wherein I would begin the next two years of my life.

CHAPTER TWENTY THREE

A TTENDING AN ALL-GIRLS Catholic college that was co-ed at night definitely had its advantages. Aside from the overall aesthetics of the vast amount of women parading across the campus between classes, there were also class sizes, student to teacher ratio, and all the classes I'd taken wherein I was the only male and was constantly asked for the "male" perspective on the situation. Each and every time I was put into this situation, I had one of two choices. I could be honest, depending on the situation, and tell these barely legal adult young women how truly disgusting and sex driven men really are. And depending on the extent to which a man has a chance of getting laid would depend on his choice of response and/or action. Or, I could give them exactly what they wanted to hear, which more times than not, was the perspective of choice. This way, I was able to have women approach me after class, so as not to feel like a social leper, find study partners for exams, and get notes from classmates in case of my absence from class. Even though this sounds like the wrong thing to do, I had my reasons. And they weren't sexually motivated, at least not the majority of the time.

Making friends has not always been an easy thing for me to do. I was an extremely shy child and would become nervous to the point of almost becoming sick when placed in a social situation wherein I knew no one. Contrary to popular belief of my friends and family, I am still this way, even today. I don't really enjoy social situations as much as the people I know would think and would truly rather stay home and just read a good book. Most of my friends consider me the life of the party, but for me that's easy once I already know people. Strangers are a different story, and I find that I have an especially hard time socializing with women. Therefore, I was incredibly angst filled upon beginning school at this less-than-prestigious institution. Also, I might mention the fact that my appearance at times could be quite frightening making the overall situation even worse at times.

People tend to judge a book by its cover and knowing that you only get one chance to make a first impression, I was very careful about how I dressed for the first month or so of school. Always having the right designer clothes and feeling comfortable in such, I was careful to always wear long sleeve shirts. This was quite a challenge for the first month of classes during the fall semester, being that it was still summer-like weather, but I was able to pull it off without a hitch, and impressed myself while accomplishing such a feat. Ridiculous as it may sound; my reasoning for this alliance with long sleeved shirts at the end of summer was for a very good reason. Believing that society tends to judge one's appearance, I felt it in my best interest to remain low on the radar and not show the various tattoos which covered the length of both my arms, thereby hopefully not having anyone prejudge me before they got to know me. Sad as this seemed to be at the time, once I got to know the women in my classes and they saw my arms, they seemed slightly taken aback and were surprised at the amount of work I'd had done. When asked whether or not they would have been so inclined to approach me and talk to me had they seen them before getting to know me, more than the majority of them were honest and said probably not. In hindsight, I'm glad I handled things the way I had but am slightly disappointed not only in myself for not comfortably being me, but with the women who said they wouldn't have probably talked to me, proving that we do, as humans, tend to judge a book by its cover.

Throughout the next two years that followed, I made a few good friends, networked numerous connections in regards to my profession, dated here and there, and was able to graduate with better than average grades. Through hard work and perseverance, I truly deserved everything I had worked so hard to achieve. Sitting at my commencement ceremony, I remember being more proud of myself than I had ever been before. With my family in tow, I remember the look on my parents' faces as I was called forth to receive my well-earned diploma. It was one of sheer and utter pleasure and it will be a long time before I will ever relinquish that memory. It was a totally perfect day, except for one small thing. While waiting to be introduced as the undergraduate graduating class of 2001, the commencement speaker finishing her speech, the administrative officers from the college first called up the students who had earned their master's degrees. I immediately wondered if what I had accomplished was enough.

CHAPTER TWENTY FOUR

I T WAS A Monday morning, around ten, when I arrived at the library of Yarseville High School, fully prepared and excited to take on my first full year of teaching. About ten days before the start of the scholastic year and Miss Hayleigh had organized a, what I thought was mandatory yet came to find out later was not, meeting of the new hires in the English department. One of the first to arrive, I was greeted by Miss Hayleigh with exuberant enthusiasm and excitement.

"How are you, Jared?" she asked in an invitingly warm manner.

"Very good, thank you, yourself?"

"Excited! We have a superb bunch of new teachers in our department this year and I'm really looking forward to all of you working together. Today's meeting should be fun."

Fun? What the hell was going to be fun about the realization that over the next ten months, I would be lucky if I had time to go to the bathroom? Leery about her, what I thought at the time to be over-the-top enthusiasm, I took a seat next to one of my fellow new hires I would be working with over the next three years.

"Hello there." said an overly pretentious looking, school-marm dressed, twenty year old who I would later find out completed her four year teaching degree in three years and had in her possession more bags and books than I assumed I would have ever used throughout a whole year of teaching, "My name is Margaret Minson, and I'll be teaching junior and senior English this year. What about you?" Barely able to reply to her inquisition, she again chimed in to tell me that she would be the editor of the newspaper and hoped to start a medieval renaissance club here in the school.

"Great", I said with forced enthusiasm, wondering if the other hired individuals in our department would have just as little in common with me as I now realized she had. Trying desperately to be cordial, I briefly discussed with her where we were both from as well as the colleges we attended when in came the other three new hires. I remember watching them as they walked through the library doors, that they sort of made and entrance as if they were in a "Charlie's Angles" movie. Relieved at there arrival, if not to get the meeting started, than just for the simple fact that Margaret would hopefully stop talking. I would soon come to find out that she, Margaret, was to be the X factor in the meeting. That meaning that she was the one individual, the one who attends every meeting I have ever been to, that seems to feel the need to speak in order to hear herself talk. Nothing prudent or meaningful is usually ever said, ridiculous questions are asked, so as just to cram one's nose up the person in charge's ass, and take a two hour meeting and extend it at least another hour. Assuming that this would be her mode of operation throughout the entire meeting, I kept my questions and comments to a bare minimum, in order to leave the meeting before sundown.

As the three new girls made their way to the table and took their seats, Miss Hayleigh instructed us to introduce ourselves to one another and then we would get the meeting underway. Sonya Johnston was a slightly round faced young girl, about twenty-two or twenty-three, with long straight, dark hair that came down to her waist. She looked tired and worn, much older than her years, and was plainly dressed, bearing not a ounce of make-up. She carried a yellow legal pad in one hand and a blue ball-point pen in the other. When she spoke, it was barely above an audible whisper. She seemed a bit nervous and spoke only when spoken directly to. Very quiet and reserved in character, I would later come to know her and find out what a hard-working, nice person she truly was. She was the teacher whose position I took upon being hired, therein changing her schedule around, teaching a variety of different sophomore and freshman classes which she would later come to hate, constantly mentioning to me that she wished she was teaching the original schedule Rachel had given her. Over the next three years, Sonya would become sick, on and off, with her cancer coming in and out of remission, but worked diligently, always keeping her students' best interests in mind. Upon my departure, she was still employed and was getting tenure and I'd hoped she reconsidered staying in this district, for it was having severe lasting effects on her, both mentally as well as physically.

The next teacher to introduce herself was Veronica Fuhrlong, a recently relocated southern girl who spoke slowly as well as soft, with a distinctive drawl to her speech. She was appropriately dressed in a flowered skirt, small heeled shoes, her long auburn hair flowing down just off of her shoulders, and glasses. She looked quite studious, portraying the look of a professional and was very sweet and endearing when she spoke. Adamant about her convictions, she had a way of getting slightly boisterous and defensive upon speaking on topics in which she truly believed. Her classes were compromised of freshman, sophomores, juniors, and seniors, and would eventually become the girls' varsity field hockey coach. Although shy and somewhat reserved, she was a sincere young woman who I repeatedly watched throughout our working relationship together, get taken advantage of. This saddened me on repeated occasions and I wished something better for such a nice young person. She would later marry and during my third and last year of teaching in Yarseville, you could see this place had emotionally taken its toll on her. During our last conversation together, she mentioned her and her husband wanting to have kids and they were going to begin trying that up and coming summer. I hope for her sake, they were successful in their endeavors.

The last of the three women to give their own introduction was very different from the latter. Dressed smart as she was, I would come to find out that she would only be with us for that year. Impeccably garbed in a designer business suit, with matching shoes, she was over-confident yet very nice. Her maturity level left a bit to be desired and as the year went on, I would hear students in the hallways discussing how Ms. Portis monopolized the majority of that day's classroom discussion with conversations about the cost of her boots or her handbag. Even in the meeting, during one of the breaks, I overheard Rachel and Ashley, Ms. Portis, discussing shopping for clothes and their outfits which they were wearing that day. I generally found her to be a nice person, attractive, but personality wise definitely not my type. Now that's not to say that I entered this meeting looking to find a date, but as a person, we, she and I, were very different.

It eventually came time for my self introduction and the meeting finally got underway. We discussed teaching styles, behavioral scenarios, and worked on a mock lesson plan, thereafter, reviewing a partners' work and critiquing it both positively and negatively to our peers. About two and a half hours in, a young woman in what I rightfully assumed to be in her mid to late twenties was introduced to us by the name of Kate Michaels. She entered the library haphazardly dressed, with cutoff jean shorts, white Keds sneakers, a grey, t-shirt with no print or defining marks, and barely any make-up. Her 1980's mullet haircut was barely disguised by the oversized yellow scrunchie which held her pony tail in place atop of her head. Upon her introduction by Rachel, we soon realized Kate to be a third year teacher who voluntarily came in that day to talk about our department as well as the school and sing the praises of our new boss, Miss Rachel Hayleigh. She carried with her three enormously, oversized binders, each marked with a class level on the outside. Immediately, she began telling us all about what a pleasure it had been for her to have the opportunity to work in such a wonderful environment, especially for such a wonderful supervisor as Rachel. Blushing slightly, Rachel immediately returned the compliment saying what a hard worker Kate has been. After about twenty or so minutes, Kate discussed how the English department was like a family, wherein everyone shared everything and was willing to help one another for the betterment of the students. I couldn't help but feel elated at the time, wondering if I hadn't in fact chosen the perfect fit for me as an educator.

Upon completion of Kate's information session, we all adjourned and were to meet at a local pub down the road about a mile. After thanking both Kate and Rachel, I gathered my things and made my way out into the hallway, in search of my car wherein I was in desperate need of a cigarette. Making a wrong turn, I was forced to double back once I reached the gym, realizing I had gone the wrong way and was approached alone by Kate.

"So, what do you think about Yarseville so far?" she asked playfully.

"Seems interesting," I said, not wanting to give off that ridiculous, "I'm so excited to be a new teacher in my first year in this profession" aura.

"You'll love it!" she said, eyeing me up and down the whole time she spoke.

"A few of us from the department are going out tonight for some drinks if you're interested. A place called Callaway's, right down off of Main Street. I'd love to show you around."

"Thanks all the same", I said in an appreciative tone, "But I already have plans for this evening." knowing that not to be the case. "Maybe next time", and was on my way, now even more in need of a cigarette than I had been before.

Once inside my car, a breathed a sigh of relief that the meeting was not only over, but that I was able to avoid the obviously forthright advances of the neediest individual I would ever come to meet during my three years at Yarseville. I learned a long time ago never to date anyone you work with. "Don't shit where you eat!" was the way it was originally conveyed to me many years prior, and I up until that time was able to live by this creed. That was, however, until my second year . . .

CHAPTER TWENTY FIVE

I T WAS A Thursday morning, the week
before Labor Day Weekend, and all of
the staff members at Yarseville High School were assembled in the school's auditorium.
The next two days would be filled with brief "how to" sessions for new teachers and
the majority of the days left for individuals to gather their books and any other items
they needed, as well as prepare their rooms for the up and coming school year that
was just about upon us. Seated alone in the fourth row, center section, left side of the
large 800 seat theater, I soon learned we were waiting for Superintendent Thistle to
arrive and greet us with his opening year greetings, comments, and well-wishes. This
unexciting turn of events was brought to my attention by Doris Martin, art teacher
who had previously bestowed a yearbook as well as her opinions about my new
co-workers upon me. I was glad that she had felt comfortable enough to come and
join me, especially since I was new and virtually knew no one, except for the new
hires in my department, none of which I had yet to see arrive. She told me how glad
she was I took the job and immediately I was engulfed in her unforgettable scent of
decade old perfume, as well as her pessimistic opinions on entering staff members.
"This sucks!" I remember thinking to myself, having the town crier chewing my ear
off about whom she didn't like and why, on my first paid day here. Wanting to get
away from her so as not to have a direct association with someone who was probably
not looked at in a favorable light by my colleagues, I was forced to just sit there and
ride it out. Thankfully, just moments later, Margaret entered and sat down next to
Doris, introducing herself after greeting me and proceeded to drone on to her about
herself right up until Superintendent Thistle arrived, thereby relieving me from my
utter dismay.

Sitting as close to the front as I was, I would come to question my vision of what it was I was about to see. Waiting to be announced by Principal Black, as if he were a national celebrity of sorts, Superintendent Thistle remained unseen until his introduction. He walked in from the left side entrance nearest the stage, looking like what I can only describe as a complete ass. At first sight, I truly believed I was imagining things. Sauntering in with a holier than thou attitude, he couldn't have looked more ridiculous if he had tried. Using his authoritative, lower than normal voice which I was privy to hear during our initial meeting with one another, he paced back and forth across the front of the stage, verbally relaying his expectations to his employees. He was dressed in what I could tell to be the same faux leather cowboy boots, denim jeans that were so pressed and stiff it looked as if they had a cardboard lining, and a black leather motorcycle jacket. As if the jacket, which remained zipped up and on throughout the duration of his pontification, wasn't enough, he actually carried around his motorcycle helmet under his left arm, the entire time. "Guess he wasn't driving the Corvette today", I remembered laughing to myself. "Was this guy for real?" I thought. "Why the hell didn't he leave the helmet and take off the jacket? What was he trying to prove? And when the hell did Marlon Brando become our superintendent?" Chalking up his ridiculous attire to low self esteem and the need to feel important, I sat attentively smiling while my top boss verbally as well as visually made a fool of himself. He spoke of the importance of a child's education and our responsibilities as teachers to uphold certain standards. "Exactly my sentiments", I thought; then went on to tell us that every one of us should give the students homework that night. "Strange how I would later come to find out this man was never even a teacher, yet felt compelled to tell us all how to go about doing our jobs. Eventually, after what I can only assume as his tiring from walking back and forth across the stage with that ridiculous jacket on, carrying his helmet, he wished us all good luck in a condescending, "you'd better heed my warnings or else", tone and left. The only thing that would have made his entire presentation more ridiculous would have been if he rode off the stage on his motorcycle with an overweight and balding Dennis Hopper by his side.

Directly following Superintendent Thistle's "guess what kind of automobile I came to work today on" game of charades, we were introduced to the administrative staff, department supervisors, and their introductions of the new hires within their respective departments. Paying little if any attention, due solely to the reason that I was still in utter disbelief at the realization that I was actually working for someone as ridiculous as Thistle, before I knew it, the meeting was over and we were to break up into our departments. Herein, the new hires would again be introduced interdepartmentally.

Hustling out to my car to have a few drags of a cigarette, I quickly made my way back into the building for our departmental gathering. Entering the room with the majority of the teachers from my department, I found a seat in a row about halfway back from the front of the room, nearest to the door. Therein my thoughts on choosing this seat was to not seem too anxious and excited by sitting in the front, while alternatively not seemingly like "the bad kid in class" by sitting in the back. The meeting began with Miss Hayleigh welcoming everyone back from their summer siesta then having everyone briefly introduce themselves as well as their specific subject matter within language arts. Basically, from what I could surmise at the time, this was for the benefit of us new teachers. Looking around the room, I remember being shocked at how large our department was. There were approximately twenty-eight teachers in our department alone. Upon the conclusions of introductions, Rachel began telling the entire audience what she expected from us this up and coming year, wished us well, and then dismissed us all to begin work on setting up our classrooms. But before we were dismissed, she asked that the new hires stay, as well as their mentors. "Mentors?" I thought. "Who the hell said anything about a mentor?"

As the smoke began to settle from the barrage of teachers making their way out into the hallway, I carefully monitored which veteran teachers were staying behind, wondering who my mentor would soon become. Then, just when I took a moment to look at the clock's time above the door through which we entered, there was a tap on my shoulder and to my surprise, stood before me a short dark-haired older woman who immediately introduced herself to me as Ms. Elsie Veranski. Upon closer inspection, I noticed her to be an old, as opposed to an older woman, with short dark hair, leathery tan skin, liver spotted hands, and the most ferociously terribly breath I had ever experienced in my life. I remember cringing on the inside when she greeted me with a rub on the back and a closer than normal invasion of my personal space. "What luck", I thought. Someone's decrepit old grandmother with extreme halitosis and personal space issues was going to be my mentor. Politely as I could, with tears just about welling up in my eyes from the stench emanating from her mouth, I reached out and shook her hand as if excited at the opportunity to work together. Up until this exact moment, I had no idea that I was going to have a mentor and couldn't imagine the purpose of one. Miss Veranski quickly motioned for me to follow her, informing Rachel that we were going to her classroom to get started familiarizing me with the workings of my new academic environment. "Have fun", Rachel quipped, and before I knew it, I was sitting down face to face with my new mentor and eventual saboteur here at Yarseville High School.

CHAPTER TWENTY SIX

WORKING THE PAST five years in education, in a special education environment to be exact, I quickly came to realize what a caddy profession teaching can be. Now that is not to say I am stereotyping, but, the majority of this profession is comprised of the female gender and at times, the worst feminine qualities can come out and remain evident on various different levels, even in men. A majority of the men I have worked with have even developed this innate ability to complain and gossip about everything and anything, almost as if it were a second profession of theirs. Unfortunately, this is how the profession is, and not being like this, I was to pledge to myself that on my maiden voyage as a full-fledged, certified teacher, I would never allow myself to get caught up in what I found to be completely juvenile and irresponsible, as well as grossly unprofessional.

My theory on education is and always has been simple. Give your students what they need to succeed in life. Why else would they come to school? Understanding and succeeding within the academic curriculum is a necessity I will not disagree with. However, I truly believe that a school's hidden curriculum is just as, if not more important than its academic one. That being that socialization skills and the ability to take what they learn academically and apply it to real life surroundings is my main goal for my students. I remember my days in high school when the majority of my teachers treated me as well as my classmates as if we knew nothing. We were taught what we needed to know, as mandated by the state or some higher educational entity, rarely ever realizing why we needed to know what we were learning or having any guess as to what practical uses those learned materials would have later on in life.

At the time, this to me seemed a poor way to teach and reach the minds of young individuals. Young people like to be told the truth, and to be given the opportunity to make choices without the hand of an adult forcing a decision on them. How else will they ever learn from their mistakes if they are never given the opportunity to make choices for themselves? I have made a vast number of mistakes throughout my life and cherish every one of them. By learning from them, it gave me the skills to better adapt myself in order to better handle a situation should one of similar experience arise. So my style became quite simple. My methods, though odd at times were extremely effective. I would teach English from a vocational aspect, challenging my students to uncover why they needed to know the materials we were covering, and eventually surmise as to how they could apply these skills to life. Therein making themselves better equipped young individuals, eventually ready to go out into the world possessing the skills in which they would need to succeed.

I found that engaging students to learn English subject matter to be quite challenging. My goal was to make my students challenge themselves and think outside the box, wherein, they would surprise and impress the one person to which it would really matter impressing; themselves. Throughout my three years teaching in Yarseville, I was considered by most to be a bit too unorthodox, to say the least, and I believe that on various levels, this, coupled with the vengeance and jealousy of various staff members, eventually led to my leaving this district. I taught classes outside, organized writing exercises in the snow, took field trips within the building, orchestrated reenactments of plays in the auditorium in full costume, allowed students to stand on their desks, and the language flowed freely in my room. Now the majority of my colleagues as well as administrators took great issue with the last mentioned detail, however, when teaching English, I would encourage my students to express themselves in a manner in which they felt comfortable. This did not mean that we would sit around the room and use nothing but profanity. But I felt that to truly express oneself, one cannot be given limits as to how to do so. Therefore, I allowed my students free vernacular range when it came to expressing themselves, as long as it was in reference to the topic work at hand. I found them to appreciate this style of me letting them be themselves and rarely was there a time when I had to speak to a student about inappropriate language being used out of context. This gave them the opportunity to be responsible, not only for themselves, but to others around them. I still believe this to be an effective method of teaching and use it to this day. I enjoy teaching immensely and find great comfort and joy in my students' success. Having your students like you as a teacher and trust in you as a confidant is a major responsibility, one which I have never taken lightly. I never entered into this profession to make friends with my students. My students are my students and always will be. I will care for them always and want the best for each and every one, looking to them as our future. Teaching has never been a popularity contest and whether or not my students liked me never really mattered. Sure, if they liked me it made my job a lot easier and much less of a headache, but that was never a concern of mine. Thankfully, I was lucky enough to have a good rapport with the majority of my students and they understood that I was there to help them. "My paycheck stays the same whether or not you pass or fail", I used to tell them, attempting to convey to them that they needed to succeed for themselves and no one else. Unfortunately, in regards to my popularity as an honest, forthright teacher with the students, many of my colleagues despised me and my heightened popularity quickly began to work against me.

CHAPTER TWENTY SEVEN

O NCE SEATED IN Ms. Veranski's room, she immediately joined me, sitting directly across from me at an adjacent desk, and began asking me what I thought about everything thus far. "I think you need a friggin' breath mint, lady", was what first came to my mind, however, I thought better of using that comment during our first meeting together and replied with an overly enthusiastic, "Excited but nervous. There seems to be an awful lot to learn and you don't really have a lot of time to learn it."

"Don't worry", she replied. "You'll be fine. Everything will fall right into place and if you have any questions, come and ask me. That's what I'm here for, right?" Her reply, still hanging in the air, as if suspended by one of those word bubbles you see in the comic section of the newspaper, I couldn't help but wonder what she meant. Lost for a moment in my own thoughts about what she was saying, I was jarred from my daydream by a knock at the door. As she motioned for the visitor to enter, I noticed a tall, extremely balding older gentleman, who looked as if he were very agitated, entered the room.

"Elsie, I'll be downstairs in the office when you're finished here", he said to her, looking at me with contempt and disgust. "How much longer are you going to be?"

"I'll walk down with you now Jerry", and proceeded to instruct me to make myself at home in her room, which I earlier that day had found out would be one of the three rooms I would be sharing with a fellow staff member. She quickly rose from her seat and walked out without another word. Jerry Galler, long time history teacher and employee of Yarseville High School, immediately exited the room without so much as a hello and proceeded towards the office without waiting for Elsie. I found him not only to be rude and obnoxious, but lacking people skills as well. "What the hell kind of a person doesn't excuse oneself when interrupting a conversation and doesn't even greet one of the members of the party he has interrupted?" I wondered. Aside from his less than welcoming demeanor, his voice was low and croaky. It was almost as if he had a perpetual frog stuck in it. I too noticed the look of distress on Elsie's face when he entered, that being of sheer horror. "What was she afraid of? Was this guy her husband?" I wondered. And in a moments notice, they were both gone and out of sight.

Wondering what strange turn of events had just taken place, Kate Michaels poked her head in the door and asked how it was going.

"So far so good", I replied and immediately found myself asking her about the tall, balding man with the croaky voice.

"Oh, that's Jerry Galler. He's a history teacher here and Elsie's adulterous lover."

"Lover?" I thought. I couldn't imagine anyone even kissing this decrepit old fossil with her offensively bad breath much less make love to her.

"Supposedly, they have been having an affair for over ten years. Everyone knows about it. He's still married, as is she, but her husband, who from what I've heard is gay, sleeps in a different bedroom than her and they have sort of an understanding."

What this understanding could be I could not have even ventured to guess so still being awestruck as I was about this disturbing tidbit of information I'd just received, the only reply I could muster was, "Interesting".

"Wanna grab some lunch?, Kate asked, reeling me back to reality and thankfully removing the thought of those two teachers engaged in a naked embrace from my mind, I without thought said, "Sure", and we were off in her truck, happily smoking what I felt at the time to be a long needed cigarette. As we made our way down Main Street to a small pub about a quarter of a mile away, my mind began to drift.

Unable to recall any of our conversation on the ride over, I noticed during the brief trip what an utter state of disarray her automobile was. There were empty cigarette packs strewn across the passenger side of the car's floor, papers haphazardly thrown upon the back seat, various bags and pocketbooks, all just cast aside as if they served no real purpose except to disorganize the life of someone whose life I would come to find out was in need of no further disarray.

Once inside the pub, we ordered lunch and she immediately began to tell me all about herself. "Great", I thought. Here's another loon from the loony bin, verbally spewing out their life story to me as if I even gave a shit. I listened attentively about how she was recently divorced, lost a lot of weight, loves her job, loves the kids, loves her new apartment, loves her cats, was excited about getting tenure this year, and how she just wanted to go out and have fun now that she was single. Fearing the last of her ranting topics of conversation to be followed by another invite which I was at the time determined to turn down, I immediately interjected, saying that my girlfriend and I, a complete conjured up figure of my own imagination, liked staying home and being home bodies. My attempt here at fiction was in hoping to deter any further advances from this desperately in need of attention young teacher. Although seemingly sweet on the surface, Kate had a knack of playing both sides of the fence. Meaning, she too was a queen of gossip and would sell you out just as soon as look at you in order to gain acceptance and find a commonality between her and her peers.

After lunch and thankfully having abruptly stopped her advances with the fabrication of a non-existent girlfriend, we drove back to school. She continued, speaking on incessantly about God only knows what, while I just nodded my head in agreement, counting the seconds in which our conversation would finally be terminated. Back inside the parking lot, I thanked Kate for the invite to lunch and headed back into the building. I told her I would see her around, leaving her inside of her truck to smoke one last cigarette before returning to work.

CHAPTER TWENTY EIGHT

T HE REMAINDER OF my first paid, non-student day consisted of me collecting the required books for my classes, setting up my grade book with the list of students' names provided to me late in the day by administration, sorting through without any direction the mountain of paperwork consisting of rules and responsibilities of teachers at Yarseville High School, constructed and put together class folders for each section I was to be teaching, fine tuned my first week's lesson plans and decorated the small square bulletin board left to me by Ms. Veranski, wherein, I drew a three dimensional box in black permanent marker with a dot inside and an arrow pointing to it from outside its boundaries, with the phrase "You are here" adjoining the beginning of the arrow. The above caption read, "Now do something about it!"

As the day grew later and the sun began to set, I couldn't help but notice how empty and void the school was of teachers. "The first day of school is fast approaching", I thought, wondering how just about everyone but myself and a few others could have left so early. Realizing the late time of day, I quickly organized my materials on the shelves provided to me and made my way out into the hallway and downstairs to the parking lot. On my way out of the room, I was stopped in the hallway by a teacher in the next room who introduced herself as Mrs. Valerie Littleson. She was a round, older than middle-aged woman, impeccably dressed in a navy blue one piece dress, with a scarf tie loosely around her neck, draping over her shoulders. The design of the scarf, as best as I can recall was of red and blue paisley, perfectly fitting in color as well as in regards to an accent piece for her outfit. It was fastened in the front with a gold indistinguishable broach and opened and spread out in the back, coming to a point just above the middle of her back. She immediately reminded me of my own high school English teacher Mrs. Merna.

"And who might you be, young man?" she asked in a tone resembling that of motherly authoritativeness.

"I'm Jared Whitmore, new English teacher this year. It's a pleasure to meet you."

"Oh Jared, I'm so glad I found you today. I had an early morning engagement that ran longer than I had initially anticipated and hoped we would be able to meet before the first day of school. Seeing as how I won't be here tomorrow, I wanted to welcome you and wish you luck your first year here at Yarseville. Also, Rachel informed me that you would be sharing my room with me and it always excites me to work with new staff members. Come on in and I'll give you the dime tour." Still shocked as I was that Rachel had not told me I would be working in different rooms at different times, having found out my situation earlier in the day from Kate, I guess in hindsight it all made sense. Being that if I was only in Elsie's room all day, where then would she be teaching?

"Thank you", I responded in a respectfully professional tone and followed Mrs. Littleson into her room. For the duration of our conversation, she did most of the talking while I respectfully did most of the listening. She spoke with perfect grammatical dialect, almost priding herself on it, and was very direct and to the point about how she did things here at work. Polite and courteous throughout our entire exchange, I would come to respect this woman over the next six months, wherein she was then retiring, moving to North Carolina, to be closer to her children and grandchildren, with her husband. She expressed her excitement at being able to focus the majority of her time upon retiring on her favorite past time, gardening. Although she frightened me a bit the way a mother does a son who gets caught misbehaving, I was glad I had met her and looked forward to us sharing a room together.

The drive home was slow but steady, possibly in part due to the fact that I was excitedly daydreaming about the adventures that lied ahead of me, and partly because of my growing fears about working in this environment, which I would come to realize would only get worse.

CHAPTER TWENTY NINE

W ORKING IN A majority populated female profession definitely has its advantages. The female to male ratio is substantially one sided and makes for a usually aesthetically pleasing daily experience. However, it also comes with distinct disadvantages as well. Speaking only for myself but assuming that the majority of male teachers would have to agree with me, the most predominant fear of a male teacher would be that of being wrongfully accused of inappropriate sexual misconduct. Thankfully, this has never happened directly to me, but I was on repeated occasions subject to witnessing this exact infraction taking place while working in Yarseville. And not only were the offenders male, but there was a female teacher incident as well.

Maintaining professionalism in my daily interactions with students, I understand that some students develop crushes on their teachers. Hell, I had the worst crush on my sophomore high school English teacher and used to fantasize about her daily while sitting idly by in her class, wondering what it would have been like to know and experience her on a more intimate level. But thankfully, she never acted on it, knowing what responsibilities her job entailed and being responsible for her actions or those she didn't act upon. Now this is not to say that she was interested in me and did the right thing, or even knew about my crush on her for that matter, but to a fifteen year old student enamored by his or her teacher, how that teacher responds or acts towards that student could have lasting effects on them, wherein there could be long term ramifications set in motion that are sometimes irreparable.

I remember about five years after I graduated high school; a somewhat new history teacher employed there was accused of having sex with a sixteen year old student on the desk in what I can only vaguely recall to be the social studies office.

After years of debate as to whether or not he was guilty and having his name and reputation splashed across the front page of the local newspapers, he was suspended with pay, the case eventually went to court. The staff therein was divided as to his guilt or innocence, and the girl who accused him was eventually found out to have fabricated the whole turn of events. It was later learned that she had a crush on him and was upset because he did not return her advances. Never having met the man but knowing his wife who was a past teacher of mine, I can't imagine the difficulties their relationship endured. And even after his name was cleared and his position was reinstated, there were still a number of his colleagues who refused to talk to him and avoided his presence completely. All because of a spurned sixteen year old, frustrated at the thought of her teacher not feeling about her the same way she felt about him. I have to be honest and tell you that upon my first hearing about the story, years before I was a teacher myself, I was disgusted by this man's behavior and had already convicted him on the mere accusations that were dealt him. Having since found out more details about the story, I not only feel terrible for this man, his wife, and their children, for the stigma that will now follow him around for the rest of his life even though he was completely innocent of any wrong doing, but also ashamed, at my immediate willingness to convict and crucify someone for something so vile before even getting any of the facts dealing with the incident.

Yarseville Battle Monument High School, as I would later come to find out, had a pension for employing individuals who were accused of such atrocities. And not only were they accused, but they were found to be guilty, for the most part unbeknownst to the parental and student communities at large, due to the fact that the three specific incidents in which I was unfortunate enough to be employed within the district while they occurred, were abruptly swept under the rug by everyone from the superintendent on down. Appalled at the thought of being employed by a district that reacted so mildly to what I believe to be a heinous a crime as any, I would eventually become fed up with this whole environment, these incidents in particular became just one of the many reasons for my departure.

CHAPTER THIRTY

E XCITED AS I was on the drive to Yarseville for my first day of teaching, I couldn't help but feel nervous. "Why?" I repeatedly thought to myself. "I'm more than prepared and everything is in order and ready to go." Thinking back, it could have had something to do with the fact that the teachers in our department, as well as those in the majority of the other departments, were working without a curriculum. In layman's terms, a basic layout as to what we are supposed to teach to our classes. When I was hired, upon the conclusion of our new hire departmental meeting, Rachel gave me a copy of each of the books I was to teach from that corresponded with each level I was teaching. She then told me to speak to one of my colleagues who were teaching the same levels and ask them what stories from each of the books were required materials. "That's odd", I thought, teaching two different freshman levels of English, five classes in all, without the vaguest hint of direction except to talk with one of your peers in order to find out what to do. I don't blame Rachel for this disorganization and lack of preparedness in this department. She is the hardest working individual in education I have ever or would ever come to know. Unfortunately, the situation was what it was and I was going to have to deal with it.

Repeatedly shaking the thoughts of nervousness from my head, I flipped down the visor and took a glance at myself in the mirror and immediately felt comforted. Dressed in tan Kenneth Cole slacks, an olive green Hirachi button down dress shirt, a yellow flowered Jerry Garcia tie with matching green and purple accents, with corresponding suspenders, and a pair Bruno Magli dark leather shoes. Comfortable, as I always need to be, in my own skin, I was ready to arrive for my first day of teaching and begin my journey to shape the minds of our future.

Pulling into my assigned numbered space on the west side of the building, I watched as the large yellow busses came and went, dropping off numerous students, all from different cultures, possessing different looks, wearing their personalities out in the open. Parents circled the parking lot in their mini vans, trucks and cars, desperately seeking a place to briefly stop and open their door if only for a second, therein unloading not only their children, but their children's friends as well. Some stopping briefly to have an inaudible discussion about how they were getting home after practice or where their dinners would be left for them upon returning from school, kissing their parents goodbye and offering a wave and a smile as they turned quickly towards the large brick building where they would spend the next one-hundred and eighty-two weekdays of the year. Others were exiting cars without so much as a word, never looking back, not even with the slightest glance, trudging their way through the beginning of their day. It all seemed so surreal to me at the time that I was captivated by the moment.

Once inside, the hallways were packed with students, running back and forth, looking for their homerooms and lockers, greeting friends they haven't seen since last school year, and staff members, milling about, making their way to their rooms, professional looking, except for the gym teachers and a few other exceptions, smiling, primed, prepared and ready to get the year under way. With satchel in hand, I navigated my way into the office, greeting my fellow workers, both of whom I already knew as well as those I would eventually come to know, with a smile and friendly and enthusiastic, "Hello". Once signed in, I was forced back out into the hallway amongst the sea of endless students, finagling my way to the first floor art room, where I would have my first day's homeroom.

The first two days of school are always different from the rest. New students and freshman are usually given a little leeway as to finding their respective classrooms for the first few days. Homerooms are extended, wherein teachers are given the opportunity to review with the students their newly acquired handbooks. This gives teachers a chance to take a breath and soak everything in, now that the school year had officially started. My first year homeroom was comprised of sophomores. The strangest year of high school I've always thought. Too old to be treated new to the environment, yet not old enough to throw their weight around due to the two older classes above them. True, they were no longer the meager and weak freshman, as they are sometimes perceived, however, aside from no longer being the new kids on the block, there were no real accolades in which to cherish. All in all, they were a lovely group of kids; respectful, polite, and extremely apologetic when they came in late. Partially due to the fact that they were just a good bunch of kids, and partly due to, what I believe, there fear of being marked late, which was barely ever an issue with me. Punctuality definitely shows responsibility, however, my philosophy after working in a special education environment with emotionally disturbed students was that I was just happy they attended.

Once homeroom ended, I made my way back out into the hallway amongst the virtual ocean of bodies, finally making it to the stairwell and hustled up the stairs to my first period class. Unfortunately, as well dressed and debonair as I thought I appeared, nothing would save me from the embarrassment of falling flat on my face, due to my misjudging the height of one of the stairs, wherein I ended up sprawled out like a deer who was just struck by a car, in front of about fifty or so students, stopping the entire procession of knowledge seekers following behind. Humbled, as I immediately became, I picked myself up off of the floor, dusted off my pants and hands, took my bag from a delightfully helpful young student who had stopped to help and ask if I was alright, assuming that upon her arrival to class, she would tell her classmates how the new teacher fell flat on his ass and looked the part of the fool, and moved forth, only too happy to arrive inside the classroom. Here I would now begin the meat and potatoes portion of my job, desperately trying to push the horror of what just happened out of my mind.

Aside from the fall in the stairwell, the first two days were virtually the same; extended homerooms, introductions of students as well as myself, review of the class rules and behavioral policies while in my room, distribution of books as they pertained to their respective level, my teaching philosophy, what the students could expect to gain from me over the next year as well as my expectations of them, a brief overview of the types of work we would be doing throughout the year, and lastly an informal Q & A session, therein allowing my students to hopefully feel more comfortable and relax in a usually unexciting setting.

Throughout my first year of teaching, I have to admit that it was an unbelievable amount of work. I still think back, even to this day and wonder how I was able to do it all. My classes were great, my students wonderful and eager to learn, and the parents could not have been more than cooperative, in terms of allowing me the flexibility and freedom to handle their children's educational futures in English as I saw fit. I am very proud of not only the work I accomplished during that first year, but in those three years combined. The two years that followed were complimented with more eager and willing students as well as understanding parents. I couldn't have wished for a better community in which to have worked and am truly thankful for the opportunity I was given to work with the students and their parents. They really made a difference in my life and taught me a lot. I respected them and they respected me in return, making for a wonderful working relationship. Unfortunately, not everything in this school was as wonderful as it had seemed.

Early on in my first year, I began to become privy to things I never in my wildest dreams could ever have imagined taking place in a school district such as this, or any district for that matter. When a parent sends their child to school, they expect that they are to be no only educated, but kept safe and out of harm's way. They also assume that the raised monies they pay in taxes upon the school budget passing go to the betterment of the overall educational experience of their children. Unfortunately, in many instances that was not the case. Unbeknownst to most of the parents and students, Yarseville High School was filled with corruption, lies, and deceit, most of which would unknowingly affect them for the rest of their lives.

CHAPTER THIRTY ONE

A BOUT A WEEK and a half into the school year, I was gathering my mail from my box in the main office, when I ran into Gary Pontier. Having been so busy this early on, I immediately realized that he was the first staff member I had really stopped to talk to since the year started.

"Hey Jared, how's everything going?"

"No complaints yet," I replied, "just trying to keep my head above water."

"Better make sure you stay low on the radar. Don't want to get on Rachel's bad side. She can be a real vindictive bitch if she doesn't like you. But you probably have nothing to worry about. Word on the street is you're her new boy wonder."

"Huh?" I replied, with a look of utter confusion on my face.

"Don't sweat it", he said. "Why don't you come out with Sandy and me after work? We're going to run over to Friday's and have a few beers. What do you say?" Feeling overwhelmed with the amount of work I not only had already accomplished so far this year, but at the amount of work lying ahead of me, I thought it a good idea to maybe stand back and smell the roses, so to say, and socialize a bit with my co-workers. Knowing already how to get to the restaurant, I replied, "Sure, what time?"

"Right after work, I'll meet you here in the office and then you can meet Sandy."

"Cool. See ya then," and made my way out of the office and back up the stairs to teach my next incoming class.

It had been a long week and I was excited by the invite from Gary. I hurriedly rushed around, picking up small scraps of paper from the floor, erasing the board, and placing forgotten books left under desks on the side shelf for students to pick up at a later juncture. Leaving Elsie's room, I gave it one last glance ensuring its state was that which I had entered it, shut the light and closed the door, desperate to shake off the chalk dust of this very hectic day. Arriving in the office, I noticed an extremely tall young woman, in what I guessed to be her mid-twenties, sitting comfortably in a matching skirt and blouse, legs crossed, as if waiting for an appointment at a doctor's office.

"You must be Jared", she said, startling me and taking me a moment to realize who it was she was talking to, "I'm Sandy Baxter. Gary has to take care of a few things and said he'd meet us there. I can drive, ready?" Perplexed at this strange turn of events, I reluctantly agreed and before I knew it we were on our way. Overconfident from the minute I'd met her, Sandy droned on endlessly about herself, actually relieving me because I could just sit there and listen without having to answer what I assumed would be another Q & A session about what my feelings were about Yarseville, being that I was a new teacher.

Finding two seats at the far side of the virtually empty bar, I immediately ordered myself a scotch on the rocks, lit a cigarette, and let the weight of the past week and a half's work and accomplishments off of my shoulders. I think that at the time, the first sip of that liquor was the best I'd ever tasted. As we waited for Gary, I was at first uncomfortable at the thought of sitting alone with such an boisterously, self-validating young woman who talked on incessantly, but after a brief time, I just sat back and listened, enjoying my drink and cigarette. Sandy spoke of how things were run, not only in the department but in the school. At one point, when I actually managed to get in a word edge-wise, I mentioned Doris Martin's name to her and conveyed the story about her giving me the yearbook and before finishing, she immediately became annoyed, saying,

"She's a bitch who likes to be in everyone's business and can't keep a secret. Be wary of saying anything to her that you don't want made public knowledge. She's married but has this huge crush on Gary, but he just uses her to buy him drinks because he's always broke. Gary wants no part of her sexually though. He's a drunk who just likes having her around because she spends money on him and he likes the fact that the attention he gets from her pisses off his girlfriend. He's dating Mindi Vaughn, one of the secretaries in the main office at the high school. I don't know if you know who she is; nasty looking, acne faced, always looks like she needs a shower. That woman actually left her husband and two kids for him and he basically pays her next to no attention at all. I can't stand her and she doesn't much like me because she heard Gary and I had a thing going last year. Well, it wasn't really a thing. I just gave him a blow job in the parking lot of this bar we usually go to every Friday after work, after we had one too many, so I guess you wouldn't say we had a thing. It was just one time. He wanted more but I couldn't be bothered. There are too many single, good-looking, available young men out there for me and I sure as hell wasn't going to settle on Gary. He's drinks way too much and has way too many issues."

"What the hell just happened?" I thought, startled at what I had just heard. "How did I get here and why the hell did I agree to come?" This woman seemed to be verbally trashing everyone she mentioned, including Gary, who was supposed to be her friend.

And why the hell did I need to know that she gave Gary a blow job? "Who the fuck tells people this shit upon first meeting them", I angrily wondered.

Trying to think of a way to get out of this place and away from this over-sexed, way too familiar, Amazon sized woman, I was just about ready to spring on her that I had an appointment and had to leave when I remembered that she drove. Screwed, and stuck there as the case was at the time, before I could let the feeling of sheer and utter disappointment set in, in walked Doris Martin, art teacher, staff basher, and Gary Pontier alcohol financier. Immediately, I prepared myself to watch these two women tear each other limb from limb. However, to my complete and total surprise, upon Sandy seeing Doris enter, she motioned her over with a big wave, greeted her with a big smile, and the two hugged and kissed one another on the cheek.

"Hey sweetie, where's Gary? He told me he was meeting you two here. Hey Jared, glad you came out." Doris said while adorning me with a sloppy, wrinkle lipped kiss that permeated my skin with the scent of elderly people. "Uh . . . hey, . . . Doris", I replied, shuddering from her repulsive scent and the fact that these two weren't beating the piss out of one another. She pulled up a seat on my right, leaving me in the middle of the two, for what was to make for a more than interesting rest of the later afternoon.

Gary wouldn't arrive until after five, and for the duration of the time I was left to be entertained by these two women pretending to like one another. I found myself to be drinking more than usual, if for nothing other than to deal with my current situation. At one point, when Sandy got up to go to the bathroom, Doris asked if she had tried to "get in my pants." Surprised, I just laughed and shrugged off her comment, leaving her to reply that she's told everyone she blew Gary last year, but he denies it and says it never happened. "She just needs attention." Sitting there for what seemed like an eternity, listening to the two of them talk bad about everyone they could think of, my mind was still in flux about trying to process what I was experiencing.

Once Gary arrived greeting the three of us, I couldn't help but stare at him, wondering what the fascination about him was. About five feet, ten inches tall, overweight and balding with a severe receding hairline, puffy cheeked, with a perpetual grin on his face, as if he knew something no one else had. He was very friendly and I would come to find out via him and our two co-workers, that Gary was the social organizer extraordinaire. He planned all the school's happy hours, retirement parties, staff excursions, and holiday and birthday parties, as well as running the football pool. A half decent guy, I thought at the time, but would later come the realization that it was all an act. Thankfully, Sandy said with verve and flair that she had a date and had to leave, as if anyone I assumed gave a crap, and asked if I was ready to leave. "Sure", I said, wishing I had left hours ago. We said our goodbyes, again adorned with kisses, and made our way back to the school's parking lot where I was parked. On the drive there, she told me about her upcoming date that evening and by the time we got to the traffic light down the street from the school; I was ready to jump out the window. Thinking better of it, I remained seated, painfully endured the rest of the ride, graciously thanked her and told her I would see her next week.

CHAPTER THIRTY TWO

T HE NEXT MONTH or so of work was unbelievably hectic; writing lesson plans then modifying them, grading papers, learning students' names, actively enforcing my behavioral rules with students who wanted to push them to the limits and see if I was serious about enforcing them, back to school night, and learning and adhering to school policies, meeting deadlines, and trying to do everything expected of me without getting into any trouble. So far everything was going off without a hitch, and would for the most part for the remainder of the year. I began frequenting Friday "happy hours" on a regular basis, therein trying to develop a good relationship with my colleagues both socially as well as professionally, when one day, Elsie Veranski, my so called mentor, asked me to if I had a minute to talk with her. Immediately, my stomach knotted up. I could only assume that I had done something wrong and she needed to tell me about it. She was in fact my mentor, not that she had acted as such, giving me only a half-assed tour of part of the building and an actually excellent method of organizing my grade book which I still use to this day. Nervously, I took a seat in one of the font row student desks and she took hers behind her desk. Sitting there behind that student's desk and she at her teacher's desk, I began to feel as if I myself was back in high school and had been asked to stay after class by the teacher so as to get reprimanded for unacceptable behavior. However, she apologized for us not getting together sooner and asked if I had any questions or if I was in need of anything. Relieved, I thanked her for being so accommodating and letting me share her room and told her that so far, I'd been very busy, but everything seems to be going well and was for the most part, under control.

"Not a problem", she said in a motherly tone. "I'm so glad to see new teachers with the drive and ambition that I've seen in you thus far and am so glad that everything is going well. Rachel mentioned to me that she has been really impressed and you seem as if you are very comfortable and able in your endeavors."

"That's great! I have to admit that when you asked me to stay and speak with you: I initially thought that something was wrong."

"Not at all. You're doing great. I just wanted to see if you needed anything and kind of touch base. Do you mind if I ask you a personal question?" "Personal question", I thought. What happened to all the "you're doing great" and "Rachel is very happy with you" talk? What was she getting at and why had the conversation turned so quickly? Not sure how to respond, I relaxingly attempted to say, "Sure, go ahead", and awaited her inquisition. With a slightly nervous look on her face, biting at her lower lip just before speaking, she looked down at her hands as if she was ashamed of what she was about to say, and asked:

"You go out to the happy hours on Friday, right?"

"Uh . . . Yeah", I replied, having no idea as to what she was getting at.

"The people who usually go, Sandy, Doris, Kate, Gary, Mindi, they're all fairly new teachers, at least within the last five years, except of course for Doris. Do you think it's a good idea for you to hang out with them as much as you do? I mean, I think you're doing a wonderful job teaching and handling all of your responsibilities, but, people in this school tend to be very judgmental. I don't want you to get caught up in hanging out with the wrong crowd. Word is they drink and do drugs and party way too much, shirking their responsibilities. I would hate to see a nice young man like you with so much promise throw it all away because you're hanging out with riff raff. I just don't want people talking about you in a, how should I say, negative light, the way they do about the rest of them. I just don't think it a good idea and hope you reconsider spending so much time with them."

Startled at what I had just heard, I tried to keep my jaw from hitting the desk from which I sat behind and said, "It's not like that. It's true that I don't know them very well and yes, I agree with you that I don't want to be associated with individuals everyone speaks negatively about. And they do, on occasion, drink a bit too much and talk about other staff members. But it's just an end of the week way to relax and blow off a little steam. It's virtually harmless."

"Just be careful is all I'm saying. I don't want people here speaking of you the way they speak about that group. I'm your mentor and I'm just looking out for your best interest, that's all."

"I'm fine, and thanks for worrying, I really appreciate it." I responded in an overly sincere tone. Assuming our conversation was finished, I rose from the desk, and she from hers. She walked around it, extending her lower lip outwards, therein giving off the look of someone who was sad and pouting, and gave me a hug. She then touched her forehead to mine and told me to have a great weekend, go and do something fun and enjoy myself. Unknowingly at that moment, I would soon realize that this was to be the last time Elsie Veranski, my mentor, and I would exchange friendly conversation. And incidentally, . . . her breath smelled worse than ever.

CHAPTER THIRTY THREE

THE NEXT TWO weeks of work would prove to be quite hectic. The students seemed to have finally come to the realization that summer had long since past, the novelty of wearing their new clothes their parents had purchased for them for school was passé, and the thrill of reacquainting themselves with friends they haven't seen since last year seemed exhausted. Their early on, eager to learn, hard working personas were now masked with frustration laced laziness and a willingness to do little if any work. Typical behavior of high school students, however it began taking its toll on the staff, especially the new ones. Margaret Minson, first year teacher and medieval/renaissance aficionado, was fortunate enough to have a room all her own and taught directly across the hall from the class I worked out of for the majority of the day. Afternoon after afternoon, I would see her in one of the student desks next to the door, grade book in front of her, talking on the black, wall mounted phone. After noticing this on more than one occasion, it seemed to be a daily ritual of hers. I couldn't imagine who she was speaking to so feverously, more so than not, seemingly upset by or with the person on the other end of the phone. Peering into her closed door one day to see if she was still maintaining her afternoon schedule, Sonya Johnston, fellow new teacher, stopped next to me in the hall and asked me if I could believe that she was calling so many parents this early on in the school year. "For what?" I wondered. Assuming initially that her better than everyone else demeanor wasn't going over well with her students. I could only guess that she was having behavioral issues with her classes. Hell, the majority of the student body she was responsible for teaching were seniors. These kids are seventeen and eighteen years old. What the hell could she possibly be calling their parents about? Just then, the door opened and Margaret stormed out. Alarmed at first, thinking she heard Sonya and I discussing her business, she stopped dead in her tracks and began speaking to us;

"Can you believe that these parents are upset that I'm calling them to report that their children aren't doing their assigned homework? They act as if I'm the one at fault, having to call them and tell them their children aren't engaging in productive academic behavior. Don't they realize the importance of their senior year's production? It could affect them for the rest of their lives. When I was a student, both in high school and in college, I always completed all of my assignments and would have never thought of ignoring my responsibilities. And these parents, don't they care about their children's well being and their futures. Slacking off at this late juncture is just unacceptable. Why don't these parents care? How can they be so cynical? It just isn't right. I even brought in some of the outfits my husband and I made for our renaissance club we belong to. I brought in a whole bag of time period clothing that he and I designed and sewed. Can't they understand how hard I'm working? Don't they care? That chain mail armor isn't light you know, and my husband was not happy about me bringing it to school to have the children touch. Its part of his costume for our biannual gatherings, where everyone is fully dressed in time period pieces, and we speak Middle English to one another while drinking port wine and dance to music from that time period. I just can't believe this. It's just plain unacceptable. I was going to dress up next week for a lesson I was teaching, but they can forget about that happening now. I already told them I would, but after having to deal with all of this, they're going to be the one's disappointed and miss out on me taking them back in time, and showing them what a beautiful young woman looks like from that era. Well it's their loss."

Suddenly realizing that she had just gone on a proper English tirade, she quickly changed direction, saying, "I need a break. I need to use the lady's room and freshen up. Oh, I just cannot imagine having to deal with this for the remainder of the school year." And with purse in hand, she apathetically apologized for complaining to the both of us and scurried down the hall to the upstairs teachers lounge, emanating a slightly annoying clicking sound as she walked to her destination.

"What the hell was all of that? I asked Sonya in a low, laughing tone, still in utter disbelief at the entire turn of events I was privy to have witnessed.

"I'm not sure, but I think she's upset", Sonya replied, laughing more so than I. "Why would she keep calling parents and get herself upset if they constantly give her grief? And does she really dress up, make clothes, and attend parties with other people who actually do the same?" she asked.

"I didn't even know they had parties like that, and now that I do, I wish I never had", I replied. "And why is she even calling parents? Hell, I teach freshman and I told their parents that this was the time for them to begin to understand responsibility and accept the consequences of their actions. I'm sure as hell not calling parents and bothering them with things I can handle myself in class. I think she is just a bit too on the straight and narrow to not call the parents of students who are non-compliant. Well, . . . to each his own, or in this case, her own. I can see this turning into a virtual nightmare that I want no part of. And if you ever see her dressed up in her full renaissance regalia, please warn me so I can prepare myself for the shock and not laugh in her face. I would feel terrible about that, but I'm guessing I wouldn't be able to hold back."

Turning to leave, I told Sonya I would see her later and was on my way back to my room to sort out the day's madness.

Upon entering, I ran into Jerry Galler, who was walking out of Elsie's room, obviously in a desperate search for her, by the look of anxiety on his face. "Hi, how ya doin'", I said to him and was completely ignored for the second time since I've seen this man, with not so much as a look or gesture. "Asshole", I thought to myself, wondering if maybe he thought he was better than me, or if I was trying to get between him and Elsie. Laughing to myself at how disturbing the thought, I sat down in the back of the room and began grading papers. Before long, I heard a familiar voice saying my name and looked up. There I found Janice Brodsky, also in search of Elsie. She mentioned that they were supposed to be meeting a bit after school and she looked everywhere but could not find her. Unsure about her location myself, I told her that I saw Jerry leaving her room in a bit of a huff. She curiously seemed a bit upset, thanked me, quickly asked how everything was going, and left. Using Janice's interruption as an excuse to end my work for the day, I packed up my things, went down to the office, emptied my mailbox, signed out, and left for a weekend of grading and lesson planning.

CHAPTER THIRTY FOUR

B EFORE I KNEW it, it was Monday morning and I was back at work. The weekend, as so many that were to follow it would seem, was now just a blur of school work and I desperately tried to muster the energy to mentally prepare myself for the day ahead. Although it was a long and tedious morning, the afternoon seemed to fly by in a moment's notice, and before I realized the time, the final bell of the day had rung and the students were out the door. "One down and four to go", I thought to myself, hoping that the rest of the week would go by as quickly as that afternoon. Packing up my things and getting Elsie's room back in order, I remembered that I was one book shy for one of my students in my second period class. Wanting to have the book for him tomorrow, I hustled down the hall to the corner room to where Janice Brodsky taught and noticing she was not there upon my arrival, left her a note on her desk asking her for the required book for tomorrow morning. Back out into the hallway, I couldn't help notice out of the corner of my eye, Sandy sitting on a desk in the back of the room she shared with Kate Michaels. She seemed to be talking to someone. It looked as if she were flirting with her feet up on the chair, legs crossed, leaning back on her left hand which was supporting the weight of her upper body from behind, twirling her hair back with her right, as if playfully trying to get someone's attention. I instantly became curious as to who it was she was acting so coy and playful with so I knocked quickly and entered the room, planning on excusing myself and asking her if she possibly possessed a copy of the book I'd just left a note for on Janice's desk. However, upon my entering the room and attempting to ask her this question, I abruptly froze, stopping dead in my tracks, barely able to speak, forgetting the initial reason I was there. This, due in fact to the reason that the individual she was acting so playful with was a student. I couldn't believe my eyes! "What the hell was she thinking? Was I seeing things? Did I just make that up in my mind? I couldn't have." I thought, seeing his reactions to her actions, as well as the way they were looking at each other. Mortified, I turned and left without a word, forcing Sandy to rise to her feet in a somewhat incessant fashion, telling her student, who she called by name, not to move, that she would be right back.

Once out in the hallway, I quickly moved at a rapid pace and entered Elsie's room, just two doors down on the same side, and quickly gathered my things, desperately trying to make my way out into the parking lot without having to talk to anyone. However, to my dismay, Sandy entered soon after me and asked me what just happened.

"Is everything alright, Jared? You came in just a minute ago like you needed something, acted as if you'd seen a ghost, and left without saying so much as a word. What's up?" she said, oblivious to the fact I was offended by her actions.

"Oh it was nothing. Sorry to have interrupted. I was just looking for Kate. I wanted to ask her if she had an extra level C book. But I can get one tomorrow, no big deal. I left a note for Janice and she's usually pretty quick with those kinds of things."

"Kate probably has one in her closet if you wanna look. She always says she needs about ten more than she has students, that way when she gets new students in her classes, she doesn't have to bother Janice for any books. If I were you though, I would stay away from Janice. I heard that she and Elsie were talking about you this afternoon in the teacher's lounge, saying that you never bring home any work on the weekends and all you do is go out and drink. They're both bitches. Just take one of Kate's books and I'll tell her you have it when she comes back up stairs. She may even be in the room now. She just went down to see what Gary was planning for the upcoming weekend. Coming out this Friday? If you want, you're more than welcome to crash at my place on Friday if you drink too much."

Immediately feeling as if I were insane, I was having an extremely difficult time sorting out what the hell had just happened. First, Sandy was sitting way too close and acting in my opinion what I thought to be unprofessional towards a student, second, she tells me that Elsie and Janice were bad mouthing me, saying I don't pull my weight around here, third, she's telling me to just take supplies from her roommate without first asking her, and last, she asks me if I want to have an alcohol induced sleep over with her this weekend. My head spinning from the vast amount of odd events that just occurred, I quickly and uncomfortably said to her that I had a doctor's appointment in about thirty minutes that I was already going to be late for, had to run immediately, and would catch up with her tomorrow, heading out the door without so much as a look in her direction to see what, if any, her reaction may have been. Mentally lost in the proverbial nightmare of what turn of events I had just experience, I briskly move towards the parking lot to my car, avoiding the office and my mailbox, assuming that whatever awaited me therein would have to wait until tomorrow, as would me signing out, for I was in no shape or mood to speak with anyone.

Inside the car, I quickly turned the engine over, threw the car into gear, and sped away; assuring myself that nothing or no one would stop me before I exceeded the town of Yarseville's city limits. Fumbling for a cigarette, I finally retrieved one from the pack and placed it in my mouth, and upon doing so, noticed that my hands were actually shaking from what it was I had just experienced. Attempting to grab my lighter, I watched it fall from my hands, as if in slow motion, bounce off my right leg and center console, landing itself on the floor underneath the driver's seat. Cursing it, as if it made the decision on its own to leap from my hand and wedge itself beneath the seat, I frantically tore open the glove compartment, haphazardly strewing everything around, looking for a book of matches that did not exist. Frustrated now beyond comprehension, I was forced to pull over onto a side street, get out of the car, kneel on the pavement, placing my head on the carpet of the driver's side floor, and reach underneath the seat to get the lighter. Once in my hand, I pulled it out and gave it a look of sheer disappointment, brushed off my pants and hands, jumped back into the driver's seat and lit a much needed cigarette.

As I sat there for a moment, partially enjoying the cigarette and partially feeling as if I had beaten the lighter in its quest to avoid me using it, I began to think about the turn of events back at school. "Was Sandy actually flirting with a student? Why was she asking me if I wanted to stay over her house this weekend? Why would Janice and Elsie talk about me not doing my work? I'd just seen them both recently and Elsie in particular told me what a good job I was doing." I pondered. Tired from the busy weekend and the day's long drawn out morning, I decided to chalk the whole experience up to me just being exhausted and assumed I would never give any of it another thought.

Over the next few months, the students came around academically and got back on track, respecting my methods of teaching and means of holding them accountable for their actions as well as teaching them responsibility. They did their work and made me more proud of them than I could have ever imagined during my first year of teaching. I worked diligently, keeping my nose clean and steering clear of trouble. I had accomplished what I had set out to do, keeping focused on my number one priority, my job as an educator to young, moldable minds. I never got reprimanded by administration or my supervisor for doing anything I shouldn't have been doing. Rachel repeatedly commended my efforts and it became apparent to me that I was in fact doing my job as an educator. On the flip side, I unfortunately came to realize that in this profession, as in any other, things would not always run smoothly. Due to what I can only assume as an overly-eager attitude as well as an excellent rapport with my students, some of my colleagues tended to dislike me and kept me a topic of conversation in the staff lounges and back corners of closed door classrooms. Uncaring as to the opinion of individuals whom I felt did not even deserve a thought, I continued on doing things my way. I kept up my fairly regular appearances with the usual Friday crowd of co-workers, finding a friend and confidant in one individual in particular. A first year science teacher named Mike Minelli, short, bald, with a carefree look on life, an affinity for beer and wine, and one hell of a sense of humor. A staunch bachelor, Mike preferred a good glass of cabernet and a Miles Davis album to any woman. As the year went on, he and I grew to become good friends and remain such even this day. We speak often to catch up and get together on infrequent occasions, but I could honestly never understand why he stayed to work in such a place. "It must have been easier to stay than to leave", I always assumed was his perspective, but to this day am still unsure. I never did stay at Sandy's house that weekend or any other weekend for that matter and my relationship with Elsie became more and more distant. I'd heard from various co-workers that she repeatedly spoke about me in a less than flattering light, saying how my teaching style was inappropriate, and that I was always hanging out with the wrong people at work. She being my mentor, we stopped meeting altogether and I was left to forge the paperwork as if we were still meeting. With only a few weeks left to go before summer, I was forced to move my things into the other room where I was teaching, and avoided Elsie's presence altogether. There was a definite strangeness between us that to my understanding, was invoked by Jerry Galler's jealousy and I felt as if I could do nothing about it. Janice Brodsky had come to me various times throughout the middle and end of the year and we spoke about how the two of them used to go out for lunch and do things together after work and now Elsie was avoiding her like the plague. She too at the time agreed that it had something to do with Jerry but could not put her finger on it. I remember feeling sorry for Janice, but as the next summer came and went and my second year of teaching began, I would come to find Janice to be as manipulative and vindictive as Elsie.

My first year ended on a good note, having numerous students tell me that I was their favorite teacher and English was their favorite class. I received phone calls from parents, thanking me for the job I'd done with their child, and glowing observations from everyone who observed me. The good well outweighing the bad and I was extremely happy. I was content to work in this district in this school for the rest of my professional career in teaching. The last day of school, my students came to visit me during periods they were not even in my class and told me they would visit me next year. Packing up after the final bell, I felt a true sense of accomplishment and inner warmth at the thought of me making a difference in so many young lives. I couldn't wait for the summer to be over to start it all again.

CHAPTER THIRTY FIVE

ABOUT TWO WEEKS before the start of school, I received a phone call from Rachel, asking me how my summer was going and if I did anything exciting. Telling her that everything was going quite well and I'd been bartending for the majority of the break, I couldn't help wonder if she could hear the desperation and excitement in my voice to begin my second year teaching in Yarseville. Acting glad that I was keeping busy and trying desperately to sound as if I was having fun, I returned the query and she replied that she was excited to begin the new school year. After our exchange of pleasantries, she mentioned the three new teachers in our department, speaking of one in particular in which she confessed was the real reason for her phone call.

"I hope you don't mind but I gave one of them your number. His name is Corbin Sampson. The two of you are going to be sharing a room and he'll be teaching the same classes as you. I was hoping you wouldn't mind talking with him and giving him some first year pointers."

Flattered and excited at the thought of beginning work early, I told her it would be my pleasure and she thanked me sincerely. Upon hanging up the phone with Rachel, I couldn't help but notice my excitement at the prospect of Rachel trusting in me and asking if I would help her out from a position of authority. "This was going to be a great year", I thought.

About two days later, I received a call from Corbin, wherein he began explaining to me who he was and why he was calling.

"Mr. Whitmore? This is Corbin Sampson, from Yarseville High School. Rachel Hayleigh gave me your number and told me to give you a call." he anxiously said.

"Call me Jared", I said laughingly. "The only Mr. Whitmore I know is my father." He replied with nervous laughter, asking me if I wouldn't mind talking a bit with him about the classes I taught last year, both of which he would be teaching sections of this year. "Listen", I interrupted, "I was planning on going up there tomorrow and setting up our room. Why don't you meet me there at about nine in the morning, we can set up the room together and I can tell you just about everything you need to know for your first day."

"Sounds great he said. I really appreciate it. I guess I'll see you tomorrow", and hung up the phone. Hanging up, I couldn't help but smile, sitting back where I'd been relaxing when the call initially came, content at the thought of teaching one of my peers the ropes.

Arriving about ten minutes late, I was casually dressed, knowing I would be getting a bit dirty moving desks and filing cabinets, hanging up posters and organizing bulletin boards, but was still able to maintain an aura of professionalism in my attire nonetheless. Once inside the main office, to my surprise I was greeted by a sight that upon actually seeing, I could not believe. There, seated in one of the waiting area chairs, sat a slovenly dressed, overweight young man. He wore blue board shorts with white trim, a white football jersey with the faded number eight in red on the front and back, and a gym bag which hung over his slumped left shoulder, where I would later find out would contain various different knick knacks, which he later placed a top his desk.

"Jared?" he asked, in voice that conveyed both nervousness as well as uncertainty. Disappointingly realizing who he was by his asking my name, he continued unprofessionally with, "What's up, I'm Corbin", and I was forced to shake his hand. "Is he for real?" I thought upon seeing his ridiculous dress and strange manner of greeting. "Who the hell goes into work looking like they just rolled out of bed from an all night fraternity party, especially to greet one of their colleagues?" I wondered. Speechless and unable to verbalize my thoughts, I motioned for him to follow me as I walked out of the office door.

"So how do you like working here?", he asked as I walked at an almost furious pace, trying desperately to avoid any association with this Neanderthal, advancing well ahead, angry with myself at the thought of having to help him, ignoring his attempts at conversation. "What the hell was Rachel thinking when she hired this moron?" I wondered.

Finally arriving at what was to be our room for the next year, I thought better of judging this proverbial book by his cover and apologized for walking on ahead, explaining that I just had a lot on my mind, asking him to forgive my impoliteness.

"No problem", he said, almost relieved, probably having known that it was actually him that I was avoiding.

"So what do you think of Rachel?", hoping that at least we would have something in common and he would think she was as wonderful as I thought she was.

"She seems really cool, but tough. I get the feeling that she hangs right over your shoulder, making sure you're doing your job."

From that moment on, the rest of the day seemed to go off without a hitch. We talked about teaching styles, philosophies, favorite authors and works of literature; he told me that his mother was a teacher and before I knew it, I was more excited than I thought I could have ever been at the prospect of not only teaching my second year of high school in a place where I wanted to work until I retired, but alongside someone else with the same beliefs as I, wanting to do what's best for the students, and willing to go the extra mile to do so. We spent the entire morning working on setting up the room, moving desks, taking filing cabinets from my room last year, organizing files, hanging posters, decorating the bulletin boards, and a vast amount of other things, all relating to school. For lunch, we drove down the street to the local pub, wherein he offered to drive. To my surprise, we jumped into a flashy sports car, one that I never would have thought him to own. Barely squeezing behind the wheel of the two seat high performance German sports car, he told me how he loved his ride and the payments were not that bad either. He said he was just an educated shopper when he leased it and had gone to the dealer at the right time.

While eating, I told him all about the two levels of classes he would be teaching that I had taught the previous year and told him I would give him a copy of my year's worth of lesson plans for him to either follow or use for ideas. We talked about the third level class we were each to teach a section of, new to me as well as to Corbin of course, and kicked around possible ideas for lesson plans and stories we could incorporate into our class. By the time we got back, we worked until after eight, photocopying, setting up our grade books, and getting everything ready for the first day of school. Watching him listen as I spoke, he seemed to hang on my every word, reminding me of myself just this past year, listening to veteran teachers give me advice. But with Corbin it seemed different. I felt as if I were watching myself in him, only I wished I had had someone as helpful as me to give me direction during my pilot year. And just as the sun began to set and we went over the last bit of first year information I could think of imparting on him, we shook hands and he thanked me for all of my help, telling me how excited he was for the first day of school.

On the drive home, I couldn't stop my feelings of utter joy and content. I was filled with a sense of happiness and purpose that I wanted to share with the world. I would eventually come to be Corbin's unofficial mentor over the next year, even though he had an official one, who incidentally, turned out to be just as if not more useless than mine was during my first year. He and I spoke a few times over the phone before the school year's start, he asking me questions and me answering what I could, and then during our last conversation before we were to begin, he said something to me that I would never forget, and would again come up later during very different circumstances. "You treated me like a brother, man, and for that I am truly grateful." Touched at the time, I would unfortunately be forced to revisit this memory with hate in my heart and a bitter taste in my mouth. For the next time I would hear it from his lips, it would be the last.

CHAPTER THIRTY SIX

I T WAS AGAIN time for the first of two non-student working days, a Tuesday and Wednesday after Labor Day, wherein the students would arrive on Thursday. Ready once again to hear the ridiculously vanity laced mantra of our superintendent, I sat back in the middle section of the right side of the auditorium with Mike Minelli, pretending to bet each other on what possible aesthetically morbid outfit would adorn his fat ass today. Mike's guess was ass-less leather chaps and a tank top, wherein I opted for the full monty, wearing only his motorcycle helmet. Realizing we were both wrong when he arrived, we both concurred he looked embarrassing and called it an even draw. Privy once again to have to sit through what I assumed would feel like a rerun of last years speech, he arrived and entered without having to be announced and, minus the leather jacket and helmet, I was thinking to myself that he may just act like an adult. Immediately, I realized how wrong I was when, during his opening welcome to everyone, he felt the need to mention that his corvette was getting new tires and his Harley was being fitted for custom leather handbags, thus being the unfortunate reason for his tardiness. Interesting I thought, being that the meeting was starting right on time and he had been standing down in front for the past ten minutes.

"Hmmm, . . . I wonder how he got here today if all of his man toys were in the shop having custom work done on them.", I whispered sarcastically to Mike.

"Guess he had to take the Bat mobile." Mike quickly whispered back, laughing to the point where he was drawing unwanted attention to himself, but quickly stopped once Thistle looked over at him, giving him a look of derision and bewilderment as to why he was being interrupted.

"Now look what you've done", I said to Mike, my hand covering my mouth so as not to be seen by Thistle as he drew nearer, "He's coming over here to eat us."

Unable to hold in his laughter, Mike immediately feigned a coughing fit and excused himself from the room in order to avoid being consumed as an appetizer. Being slightly thrown off by Mike's sudden departure, Thistle turned and made his way back towards the front of the auditorium, droning on incessantly, in the exact manner in which he did the previous year.

It was about a half an hour before Mike returned and with Thistle long since departed, I thought better of saying anything that might have made him need to excuse himself once again. Plus, the department supervisors were in the midst of introducing the new staff members in their respective departments. Just minutes before Mike returned, I was told by Doris Martin that there were close to thirty replacements this year and twenty three this year that just passed. That's about fifty people within a year's time. My first thought on the matter was that at this rate, I would be on the fast track up the seniority ladder, never realizing until much later on, what a large amount of turn over was going on in this school and why.

The meeting finally over, I ran into Corbin, who I told I was on my way outside to have a quick cigarette, when he asked me if I had an extra. Agitated, this now being the second time he asked me if I had an extra smoke. "What the hell does that mean anyway; an extra smoke. Do people that ask this assume that there are certain cigarettes in the pack that smokers deem as extra?" I wondered. Thinking better of becoming angry at his increasingly incessant need to make me his cigarette pimp, I said, "Sure", and we made our way out to my car. While outside, we briefly discussed how ridiculous Superintendent Thistle acted during his portion of the meeting, as well as some of the attractive looking new hires on this year's roster. Hustling back inside, so as not to be late for the next section of the day's activities, we inadvertently ran into Kelly Sipes. She was quite a big girl, a year or two older than Corbin, and a lifelong Yarseville resident and graduate of the school in which we were working. Kelly was another regular fixture at last years' Friday afternoon happy hours.

"Hey Sipes, how was your summer?" I asked.

"Great, yours?" she enthusiastically replied.

"Can't complain", I said, then turned and motioned towards Corbin, introducing the two to one another. As they shook hands and exchanged verbal greetings, I immediately flashed back to the first time Kelly and I ever met. It was the second or third Friday of my first year teaching, and what I would come to know as the regular happy hour crew was gathering at the local pub down the street. Only inside about ten minutes, I was seated next to Gary and Doris, finishing off my first scotch, when a round, young girl stormed through the entrance, accompanied by who I would soon come to learn was the school's librarian, Mitzy Goldberg. Opinionated and loud, Kelly pulled up a seat next to me while Mitzy took the one next to her, introduced herself and Mitzy to me in an overly boisterous tone and ordered a beer and shot for herself. She instantly began droning on about whom at work was on her nerves and how much she hated them. The entire time, Mitzy sat back and drank, shaking her head in agreement with everything Kelly was saying, but never offering up an original thought of her own. It was to be a late night and I wouldn't leave until around eleven. I remember Mitzy became so drunk that she made out with two different guys in the span of five minutes, threw up on the dance floor, and had to be poured into the back of Kelly's car, the entire time singing to anyone who would listen how much she loved them. Literally picking her up by her waist, and shuffling her under her arm, Kelly took Mitzy out into the parking lot and dumped her into the back seat of her car. Assuming she'd left to drive Mitzy home, due to her overly inebriated state, I was surprised to see just moments later, Kelly walk back into the door, saying that if she throws up in her car, she would leave her for dead on the side of the road.

As the night went on, Kelly became even more loud and drunk, and I couldn't help but wonder how she and Mitzy were going to get home. Feeling too as if I should slow down in order to make the fifty minute drive back to my apartment, I spent the next hour of the evening sitting next to Sipes, which by now was the way I would refer to her from this point on, listening to her bad mouth just about everyone we worked with, wondering if it was only a matter of time before I would be next.

Jarring the thought from my memory and snapping myself back to reality, I motioned for Corbin to get moving, so as not to be late for our meeting.

CHAPTER THIRTY SEVEN

M Y SECOND YEAR of teaching began in a very positive manner. Corbin and I were getting along infamously as roommates, sharing ideas and lesson plans, constantly being complimented by Rachel for our hard work and devotion, my new group of freshman students were eclectic and diverse, overall pleasant and willing to learn. Sophomores I had taught the previous year were constantly coming to visit me, telling me how much they missed having me as their teacher and asking for advice about everyday situations; and the Fridays' happy hour crowd seemed to have more than doubled in size. All in all, I couldn't have been happier. Although Elsie and I were by this time barely on speaking terms, due to her irresponsible attitude as my mentor and what I would come to find out to be true of her, talking repeatedly about me behind my back, I at the time just ignored her immaturity and chalking it up to jealousy or some other personal frustration she needed to deal with which I could have honestly cared less about.

On the first Friday back at work, Gary organized a formal gathering at the usual watering hole, leaving hand drawn memos in selected staff members mailboxes, inviting all those who had received an invitation to come out after work and meet their new co-workers. And by four o'clock that day, I would come to meet the majority of the individuals that I would later wish I had never encountered in my life.

I arrived early at the bar with Corbin, followed in procession by Mike, Doris, Sandy, Kate, Kelly, Margaret, Sonya, and Veronica, the last of the three mentioned attending for only their second or third time ever and eventually after only a time or two more, rarely ever going to these gatherings and associating socially outside of work again. Gary was already inside, his girlfriend Mindi by his side, drinking rum and cokes and playing a Star Wars video game, located just inside the door in which we entered. Before we knew it, various other staff members would join us making for what I remember to be the biggest happy hour gathering outside of any holiday party.

The first of the new hires to arrive was Trixie Goebles, a white trash, opinionated sorority ditz, who had a pension for liquor and an even bigger affinity for sex. Rumor had it that she would spend her summers down the beach, bedding half the male tourists and as many lifeguards as she could get her hands on. The phrase "going down the shore" took on an entirely new meaning when it came to Trixie. She perpetually looked dirty, as if in need of a constant bath, and spoke with a high pitched, nasal sounding voice that could be heard in the next county over. Loud and obnoxious, she tried to portray herself as sweet and caring, but not long into spending time with her, it was plain to see that she had severe psychological issues and would change her various psychotic moods like the weather. Her most annoying trait was her speech. Not only would her voice grate on my very last nerve, but she would begin just about every other sentence she spoke with the word "evidently", not only annoying everyone within earshot, but making her the butt of many a jokes upon her absence. For as much as I at times, more so than not, became unnerved by her entire demeanor, I couldn't help but feel sorry for her, wondering if all she really needed was a bit of unsolicited attention.

Arriving along with Trixie was Sue Jones, a dark and curly haired science teacher with man hands and never a stitch of make-up. A perpetual flirt and part time bartender, she could drink better than any guy and was known to have a slight addiction to cocaine, at times even seeming to be high at work. She was initially friendly for the first couple of months, seeming to scout out a perspective boyfriend from the coral of single studs in the stable, and struck gold when she started dating Brock Anderson, first year history teacher and hockey fanatic. She was always dressed in the oddest of manners, combining various different retro looks into the same outfit and never really cashing in on one overall theme. The irony in her ridiculous dress was that at some point during the year she deemed herself chief of the fashion police, and would constantly critique other's attire. Overall quite unattractive, but not ugly, she lacked in various areas of personal hygiene. She was sweet when talking to your face but the second you left the room, she would rip you up one side and down the other. She fit right in with this group of back stabbers immediately.

The last member of the group to arrive with Trixie and Sue was the previously mentioned Brock Anderson. A tall lanky fellow with a good sense of humor and an affinity for fun, Brock liked his beer as well as his women. A long time hockey player, and quite good from what I'd heard, he was playing one Friday night later that year and was blind side checked into the following week. The last of many concussions, he wisely opted to give up the sport. Unknown to us all at the time, he and Sue were already messing around with one another, wisely keeping their secret from the masses at work, so as not to give them any more gossip than they needed, They would eventually come out to everyone as a couple and move in together. Unfortunately, things would not work out for the best, wherein he moved out and she decided to disgrace his name by saying he was an alcoholic with a severe gambling problem who was physically abusive, none of which would turn out to be true. I liked Brock for the most part from the moment I met him, and although at times he could be a bit moody, he is one hell of a guy and we still maintain our friendship, even to this day.

The next individual to arrive was Helen Haydorn, a socially maladjusted French teacher, who was in her second year within the school. She was completely incompetent as a teacher, and from what I gathered during our few painful conversations, as an adult as well. She could be heard singing in French to her classes at the top of her lungs throughout the day, befriended students to the point that she would speak with them on the phone socially and on the internet via emails. I found her professional ethics to be repulsive. She was a homely looking girl, probably young but never cared to inquire as to how old she really was; who dressed in what could best be described as a frumpy manner. She wore too much eye make-up, kept her long blonde, bangs cut hair in the same plain fashion day after day, and drove a white T-top Firebird, a fashionably outdated car by about twenty years. From the moment I met this girl I loathed her. Not just for her unnerving voice and laugh, but from her inability to understand that while working in Yarseville, she was supposed to be teaching, and not making friends with the students. Rarely around after the first happy hour of the second year and a holiday party or two, she was eventually fired and being the mature individual that she was, wrote notes to all the people she didn't like and put them in their mailboxes on the last working day of school. Having read some of them, one would have assumed they were written by a middle school student who was mad at their friends for something completely juvenile and ridiculous. She spent the better part of an hour looking for people to corner to talk to her and singing aloud to no music. Eventually frustrated, she would leave the bar after about an hour, feeling dejected and begin storing up a year's worth of anger for just about everyone she worked with. She arrived alone and departed in the same fashion, not surprising and relieving anyone in attendance.

The next person to arrive also entered alone. Her name was Tara Saltzberg and she was a long time Spanish teacher at Yarseville. Older than the majority of the group but younger than Doris and Betty, she was thin and in shape for her age and possessed the heart of a child. Good natured and perpetually possessing a positive attitude, Tara forever looked on the bright side of things; even when there was none there to see. A lovely woman, she was hard-working and dedicated, always putting the well-being of her students' success above all else. She was a constant fixture within the school's halls and could be seen every morning and afternoon, dragging just about everything into and out of the parking lot, except for the kitchen sink. She used to joke with me that inside of her large, wheeling, black suitcase typed bag, was her worst behaved student from the previous day's classes. She was sweet and reserved, rarely ever adding fuel to the rumor mill's fire, mostly just agreeing with the newest story.

Following Tara's entrance, Bud Platt and Cecelia Summers entered and were greeted by the majority of the veteran teachers right away. Cecelia was also a Spanish teacher who was in her fourth year of teaching and she and her fiancé Bud were together more so than not. He was a sports junky and movie fanatic who had done a stint in the military, army I believe, and was for all intensive purposes, a good natured guy. He used to substitute at the high school while going to college at night to receive his undergraduate degree in computer science, and would come to be affectionately referred to as Mr. Summers by all the students. His fiancée Cecelia was a high strung ex-cheerleader who acted as if she coached cheerleading and taught Spanish as an extra curricular activity. They were a fun couple to have around, yet at times I felt bad for Bud when Cecelia would talk about him in a negative light right out in the open, saying that she wished he was finished with school and had a real job. She too was one to gossip around the watering hole and would mysteriously become angered with fellow staff members for unknown reasons, never telling that person why she'd stop talking to them; then as if nothing ever happened, resume their friendship as if everything was fine. Rarely in attendance at any of the happy hours during my first year of employment; Bud and Cecelia were at the majority of the gatherings during my second and third years.

The next group to arrive, not together yet all at the same time, consisted of Betty Moffit, J.R. Neidermeyer, and Stacy Lipshitz. The first through the door was J.R. A short, stocky little man that looked more like a student than a teacher; he was the proverbial party animal as well as a perpetual liar. Within the first two weeks of school, he turned off every single woman employed there with his adolescent advances and cheesy pick up lines. From what I'd heard, he was found out to have had sex with Trixie Goebles that following summer; something that no one was surprised about, yet shuttered imagining. His life revolved around football, wherein in his first year he became one of the lower order assistant coaches, constantly being made fun of for his lies and deceptions in regards to his being a big high school and college star, which upon his fellow coaches researching his claims, were found to be gross exaggerations on many levels. During his interview for the history position he now possessed, it was widely known that he actually attended with his mother, wherein she asked all the questions and he just sat there as if being sent to the principal's office, forced to listen to administration tell his mother what it was he had done wrong.

Betty Moffit, permanent fixture at Yarseville High School for the last thirty plus years, she had the demeanor of a clergyman's wife and the look to accompany it. Short in stature, she was somewhat overweight for a woman of her size, tending to slightly waddle like a penguin when she walked. Older than everyone else, except for Doris, by at least twenty five years, she perpetually spoke with an even keel, dressed extremely conservatively, and was even called by younger veteran teachers, "Mother Betty". However, she could gossip with the best of them, constantly passed judgment on colleagues about everything under the sun, perpetuating a state of continual complaining about how terrible the students were, and maintained the state of mind that it was 1950 and advances and changes in various arenas of academia did not pertain to her. I viewed her as the devil in disguise, a small little troll who lived under a bridge, dressed up like some church going grandmother that passed judgment on everyone and anyone she could. This is the woman who was assigned to be Corbin's mentor, wherein she did such a poor job; she actually gave him the money she was paid for doing less than nothing.

The last of the three to enter with this group was Stacy Lipshitz; an enormously tall, utterly unattractive, early twenty something year old, with extremely long, unshapely legs, an abnormally shaped midsection, the smallest torso I remember ever having seen on a human being, with arms that hung down to almost her knees. Her skin was pasty and pale, and her posture was that of someone who was constantly hunched over, bending down to get something. When I first met her, I remember feeling sorry for her because of how truly unattractive she was. However, I would later come to learn that her insides were even more unattractive than her outside. Inept at some point in developing a personality, she lived in a world where her parents thought she was a church going virgin, never having been kissed and always doing what a good girl was expected to do. I often wonder what her parents would think if they really found out what she was like. It was later brought to my attention that Stacy knew Principal Black before she interviewed with him and their relationship was the reason she acquired her current position. She had apparently gone to college with his son and they were good friends. And after seeing Stacy in action as a teacher, I can only assume that it was a good thing she went to college where she did.

The last three people to arrive all came in at different times. The first of the three was Barbara Collins, special education teacher. A robust woman in what I assumed to be her early forties, she seemed nice on the surface, but was perpetually bad mouthing people, pessimistically complaining about everything, no matter what the case. Noticeably attractive in her day, she tended to act as if she'd lost some of her edge over time and treated any female individual who was so much as cute with derision and disdain. She would on numerous occasions talk a big game, but rarely if ever followed through on her threats.

The next to last to arrive was Carla Shelby, also a special education teacher. Tall, blonde and friendly, I often felt sorry for her because of her trusting demeanor. A single mother of two teenage sons, she had the heart of a child and the willingness to help anyone in need. Unfortunately I would come to watch her repeatedly be taken advantage of by fellow staff members, especially some of her close friends. Gracious and polite to a fault, she had a strong religious background and rarely if ever used profanity, a nice young woman all around. She volunteered for various after school activities and would offer you her last dollar if you needed it. Compassionate and sweet, I liked her from the moment we met.

The last to arrive was Keith Westerbrook, Yarseville school district board of education president. Small in stature and forever dressed in professional attire, I found him to be extremely friendly. He was an overall easy going individual and a pleasure to talk to. Keith made the well being of the district a priority in his life and was always willing to listen to both parent and staff suggestions, actually doing something for the betterment of the district. Having Keith around at happy hours always made me feel as if I were given direct access the powers that be. He would always want to know how things were going at work and took a sincere general interest in staff members' concerns. Truly one of a kind, it was comforting knowing Keith was a prominent board of education member.

This was to be the majority of the cast of characters with which I would come to work with and socialize with over the next two years, save a few new hires the next up and coming year. Some positively, most negatively, all of whom would have an impact on my career in Yarseville and how I would come to look at the profession of teaching in an entirely different light as a whole.

CHAPTER THIRTY EIGHT

S TRAIGHT UP THROUGH to the winter holiday break, my life could not have been better. I'd developed good student-teacher relationships with my students and their parents, and my supervisor Rachel was more than happy with my dedication, production, and hard work. She would repeatedly thank me for what I was doing; rewarding me with first and second year college students, scheduling times to come in and supervise who she described to them as a model of teaching excellence, saying that I was responsible for the majority of the freshman class' academic success. I would later write all three levels of the freshman curriculum as well as their mid terms and final exams, and although it took up a lot of my time and dedication, I was flattered at the thought of her trusting me to take on such an important task. I became the head of various clubs and even started one from the ground up; a diversity group, wherein students were able to gather in an open forum and discuss anything from race, dress, socialization, school policies, and sexuality, to name just a few. I sincerely enjoyed spearheading this organization and with the help of board president, Keith Westerbrook, we were able to have it well on its way to becoming an officially sanctioned club. However, due to vast amounts of complaints by "old school" staff members and their strong relationships with inner school union officials, what I thought to be volunteering my time for the betterment of the school, community and well being of its students, was viewed in an entirely different light by the union. They claimed, as did various teachers who disapproved of my overly active involvement in clubs and activities that I was making them look bad and setting a bad precedent for administration to take advantage of their employees. "If I wasn't going to be paid, then I shouldn't be a part of it", was their attitude. To my complete and utter disbelief and dismay at their attitude, I could have cared less about their feelings and continued to do what I felt was in the best interests of the students. Corbin and I were actively working together, he for the most part taking advantage of my previously gained first year experience, and me feeling proud of his first year successes, taking credit for the majority of them. We began hanging out on a regular basis, telling one another our most intimate secrets. Although most people I had talked to about Corbin later on in the year felt as if he came on a bit too strong, acting initially too comfortable upon meeting them, I can honestly say that I never saw what they were talking about. We attended Friday happy hours religiously and life for me seemed as if it could not have been better.

In regards to Elsie and our previous years' falling out, I did my best to avoid her all together. Unfortunately, our rooms were directly across the hall from one another and on numerous occasions we were forced to greet each other upon making eye contact with forced smiles and imaginary pleasantries. This awkwardness was coupled with the fact that I was teaching my afternoon classes in Janice Brodsky's room, wherein on numerous occasions, she would speak to me about how her relationship with Elsie was deteriorating to a point which she believed was at the time beyond repair. I at times found myself confiding in Janice, and she in me, about some of the difficulties we were both experiencing that year. Unfortunately, our afternoon talk sessions would eventually open a door to a series of events that would drive a wedge between me and the majority of the staff members at Yarseville High.

CHAPTER THIRTY NINE

WINTER BREAK ARRIVING just days away, the regular crowd was all gathered at the usual drinking hole for our annual Christmas party. Organized, as was everything else, by Gary, it was an evening of fun and frivolity, drinking, socializing, bad mouthing colleagues, and blowing off steam in anticipation for the much needed break. It was about three hours into the party however when our host and organizer finally arrived. It dawned on me at the time as odd that he would arrive so late to a party he so successfully organized. Gary had been maintaining his job as social director with weekly football pools, happy hour Fridays, birthday parties for anyone within our social group, and making sure anyone who retired had a proper send off. However, more times than not, he was either late for his planned functions or for some reason didn't show up at all. Finding out from Doris that he was in his last semester of graduate school, about to get his certification to become a principal, I just assumed that he was busy with his studies. Although a strange thing happened the the previous week that would later come to haunt me for what it was we were all about to find out upon returning from our holiday break.

It was second period, and I was on my way downstairs to my assigned duty, when Gary stuck his head out into the hallway from within his classroom and asked me if I could watch his class for about twenty minutes while he tended to something. "Sure", I figured, assuming he had something important to do. Gary had since changed rooms from a hallway a top the library wherein no one would ever venture down accept to get to his room, to a room in a section of hallway wherein Rachel could keep a better eye on him. He and Rachel were at one another's throats, she accusing him of not fulfilling his teaching duties and him forging both lesson books and grade books in an attempt to prove her wrong. I would later come to learn that Gary had in fact forged three months of lesson plans and grades in order to have Rachel believe he was doing his work. Ironically, it was Gary who told me about the incident, finding it humorous that he believed he was getting one over on Rachel.

Thanking me as he rushed out of the room as if a man on a mission with a nervous look in his eye, collared shirt with tie around his neck, undone, as he was accustomed to have dressed, he rounded the corner and I entered his room. The students were sitting in various groups, talking quietly to one another, not doing any work, nor having direction as to the day's lessons. Greeting them with a smile, I was abruptly stopped in my tracks by what I was about to see. High above the chalk board in the front of the room, facing out towards the students' desks was a picture. Larger than any I had seen adorning any wall in the school, it was a group of senior boys and Gary, arms intertwined, he in the middle and everyone smiling. Immediately, I noticed two strange things. The first was that none of the boys had a shirt on, but were instead adorned with grease painted blue letters on their chests, together in the right order spelling out the word "SENIORS". The second strange thing was the look on Gary's face. Smiling as were all the boys in the picture, I couldn't help but notice the strange difference in Gary's smile as opposed to those of the students. It was as if there was something mischievous behind his eyes, and his smile was one of extreme excitement. Sitting in the room for what would be five minutes shy of the entire period; I found myself bothered by what hung on the wall behind me. Upon his return, I was still in a state of shock at the thought that this picture was allowed to be hung on a classroom wall. He thanked profusely, apologizing for his tardiness, and I left, a feeling of uneasiness remaining in my stomach.

Later that day, while coming back from lunch, I ran into Sandy and Kate sitting at their duty post outside the auditorium doors, just inside the school's main entrance. As I rounded the corner from the main office, Sandy called me over and told me that she had just quit and was moving to Florida to live with her boyfriend. "What? Who is? You have a boyfriend in Florida?" I thought in utter disbelief, unsure of what it was I had just heard. "Why?" I was forced to ask, not being able to control my curiosity as to the severe turn of events. And she began to tell her story; one that I would two days later come to find out was a complete and total cover up, not only by Sandy, but by the school as well.

"Rachel called me into her office this morning and told me that she has been unhappy with my work this year. She said that my lesson plans are always being turned in late and are rarely if ever up to her expected standards. She claims my room to be out of order and in complete disarray, and said she's received complaints from parents of students that I'm not teaching the required materials students need for the tests I give. And to top it all off, she said that I would be extremely disappointed upon reading her written comments on my last observation. I'm not staying around here working for a two faced bitch like her! Gary told me about all the things she has been doing to him to try and make him quit; and I should have listened to him. I fucking hate her and I'm out of here."

Shocked at what it was I was hearing, I interjected, reminding her that she was getting tenure in February.

"I don't care! I'm leaving! I already spoke to Ralph (principal of the school) and he told me that he wished I would reconsider, but understood that I needed to do what was right for me.", making it sound as if she had been railroaded and Ralph was begging for her to stay.

Still in awe, she told me she already quit and Ralph was willing to release her from her contract early, not having to return after winter break. This was something I found odd, knowing that the school would have to find a replacement for her in just two weeks time. Speechless and unable to make any type of comment, I forcibly told her I would miss her and wished her the best of luck. She told me that she would be at the happy hour later that week and couldn't wait to get the hell out of Yarseville.

Two days after the unforeseen news I received from Sandy, the truth of the matter finally reared its ugly head. That truth, although never officially confirmed to staff members by administration was as follows: Sandy never quit her job, passing on her opportunity of tenure, aggravated at the notion that she was being mistreated by her supervisor. In actuality, Sandy was fired. It became common knowledge amongst the staff members that Sandy was let go because she was found out to have gone to New York with a previous student of hers, who was still enrolled in the school as a high school senior. Not the first time they were together, he was also found out to have spent a weekend at her apartment, helping her rearrange new furniture she had ordered. Eventually, talk of the scandal reached just about everyone's ears, wherein administration concocted a remedial cover up, so as to not be held legally liable for any unseen ramifications from the aforementioned student or his parents. Appalled, but not surprised at Sandy's actions, she conveyed to everyone through telephone calls to Kate that she was using up the remainder of her sick days and would no longer have to set foot in the school in which she claimed to have forced her to quit. At some juncture throughout the development of the story being spread and the unethical attempts of administration and the board of education members trying to cover the entire incident up, I became saddened that I hadn't mentioned something to someone last year when I initially saw her speaking seductively to the young, male junior who I would eventually come to learn to be her under-aged lover. Sickened by how an adult could undermine the trust and safety of a student's well being, I was glad to have never seen her again, pondering whether she again would use her position of authority to again prey on others. As for the administration and the board of education members helping to keep the situation under wraps, I couldn't help but wonder what other devious scandals and happenings were occurring at Yarseville High School, only to be swept under the rug, therein maintaining the mask of moral turpitude and reputation for the school.

CHAPTER FORTY

THE CHRISTMAS PARTY now behind us and only an hour left in the work before break, I decided, uncharacteristically, not to attend the last happy hour of the numerical year. I had the month before booked a trip to Colorado, feeling at the time that I was in need of a change of scenery and was excited about my up and coming departure. With the final ring of the bell dismissing staff and students for their two week sabbatical and long overdue break, I began packing up my things, excited about my drive to the airport early the next morning, when Mike came into my room and asked me if I was going out for the last hoorah. Not really wanting to go but already being packed for my trip, I at the last minute changed my mind and decided to accompany Mike and the gang for one last pint of holiday cheer.

We were the first two to arrive but the others quickly followed, and by four o'clock, the liquor flowed freely and everyone seemed to be enjoying themselves. And as the evening went on, we laughed, drank, joked around with one another, wished each other Happy New Years, and eventually parted ways. Driving home four hours later in anticipation of my trip to Colorado, I couldn't help but think about why the school would cover up the incident with Sandy. Relieved that she wasn't in attendance at that evening's gathering, and contemplating the thought that her possibly being there was my original reason for not wanting to go, I instantly realized my sincere disappointed in the district wherein I worked.

CHAPTER FORTY ONE

N EVER HAVING BEEN to Colorado before, I found the entire trip to be exhilarating. My flight was at seven a.m., and I arrived at the airport about an hour and ten minutes early. Checking a single bag and reading a recently purchased magazine, I sat alone in the terminal, waiting for my flight to be called. Once aboard the plane, I anxiously awaited takeoff and afterwards, reclined my seat with my magazine in my lap, rested my head against the wall of the plane, pulled the shade, and was asleep before we reached cruising altitude. Awakened by a stewardess who politely asked me to return my seat to its original, upright position, I was relieved at the fact I had slept through the entire flight. Once off the plane, I retrieved my bag, picked up the keys for my rental car, and made my way out into the vast sea of small and midsized cars. I luckily found my rental spot within seconds of entering the lot and before I knew it was off.

It was about a half an hour's ride to my hotel from the airport and to my surprise, I was able to arrive without getting lost. I checked in at a little before twelve, thanking the clerk for allowing me entrance two hours early, and immediately unpacked.

Well rested from the three hour nap on the plane, I packed a small knapsack of warm clothes, changed from my sandals into my boots, grabbed my helmet and was back out the door to my rental car. Driving to Denver from Colorado Springs, I wouldn't be as lucky with directions as I was on the drive from the airport to the hotel. About twenty minutes longer than it should have taken me to find, I eventually arrived at the motorcycle rental shop. Grabbing my knapsack, helmet, and reservation information, I went inside to choose from the vast array of bikes, one of which I would spend the next three days riding.

Extremely friendly and helpful, I opted for a 1250, deep purple Harley Davidson Low Rider, with saddle bags and dual exhaust. It was a beautiful piece of machinery and I couldn't wait to get it on the road. After paying for the rental and insurance and reading over and signing the contract and waivers, I was ready to roll. While one of the employees was bringing my ride out of the shop and into the parking lot so I could begin my three day journey, I was given a map of the state with highlighted routes of possible travel and points of interest to visit on the way. Asking his opinion about what he felt the best day trip to be, he showed me a ride of about two hundred and twenty miles up through Breckenridge and Vail. I thanked him for his advice and told him I would be taking his suggested route tomorrow, and upon allowing me to leave my rental car in their lot for the duration of my rental, I was out the door and off to see some of the most spectacular sights in the country.

Still early in the day, I decided to ride around the city of Denver for the better part of the afternoon, taking in some of the sights from the road, and treating myself to a nice steak dinner. I was glad I'd decided to take this trip and the fact that I was alone, I was truly able to relax and enjoy myself, on my own terms. By the time I arrived back at my hotel room, I was exhausted and ready for bed. Once inside the room, I tossed my clothes on the chair in the corner of the room, took a quick shower, slipped into bed with just the towel I used to dry myself, and turned on the television, falling sound asleep before I could even realize what channel was on.

I awoke early the next morning, got dressed and ready, grabbed my knapsack of clothes and my helmet and was out the door by eight a.m. My first priority in the morning once on the bike was to find a place for breakfast. About an hour into the ride, I came across quaint little place, forty or so miles away from my hotel. The plan for the day was to eat breakfast and ride, following the two hundred plus mile route the guy at the rental shop mapped out for me. And after a meal of eggs benedict and hash browns in the rustic little diner I came across along the way, I soon noticed that the people moved at speeds much slower than I was generally used to, and was eventually off to experience the landscape and country side of Colorado a little later than I'd figured.

Starting out in Colorado Springs and having eaten at a place along the outskirts of Denver, the weather was a beautiful seventy eight degrees. Driving north for the majority of the ride, the weather would drastically change on me not only temperature wise, but precipitation wise as well. Having to stop at least a half a dozen times to add or take off clothing due to the changes in temperature, I was repeatedly forced to stop and find shelter from teeming rain on three separate occasions. Being wet and slightly uncomfortable, I chalked it all up to being part of the experience and continued on. Driving around Denver the day before, it was fun being alone in a strange city, virtually unsure of where it was I was going. However, that day's ride, even including the bouts with rain, wind and temperature fluctuations was indescribable. There were beautifully, awesome sized caramel colored mountains with various precipices, obtuse in shape, on all sides. The roads were windy and much less traveled, providing me the opportunity to proceed at just about any speed I chose and I remember making a mental note to myself to thank the guy from the rental shop for suggesting this route. And depending on which direction I was headed, the sky remained the color of light blue denim, with subtle variations of dark and light areas, adorned with cottony white clouds that danced directly on the tips of the mountain tops. I bought gasoline on an American Indian reservation, stopped for a beer at a one hundred year old bed and breakfast, located at an altitude that was higher than I'd ever been before, stopped and got coffee at a Starbucks of all places, located in a rustic old mining town and was eventually on my way up through the skiing town of Breckenridge towards Vail by four o'clock. I had already been rained three times at this point and the temperatures had dropped about forty degrees when the unimaginable happened. About thirty miles from Vail and the temperatures freezing me to the core, it began to hail. Having never actually been caught in a hail storm on a motorcycle before, I frantically searched for shelter and about a mile after the hail began falling, I pulled off the road next to an old abandoned farm house set well off of the road, boarded up and absent of any inhabitants. Quickly turning off the bike after driving underneath the awning on the dilapidated wooden porch, I tore two pieces of wood from across the doorway and shouldered my way inside. Creepy at first, I found the experience to be quite remarkable. I immediately began taking off my four layers of wet clothes, all of which I had packed in case the weather turned cold and was glad at the moment I had, and laid them out on what was left of the rotting wooden furniture, allowing them to dry out. Now down to my jeans and tee shirt, I noticed what I hoped was a working fireplace and began using scrap pieces of wood, breaking them up into kindling so as to keep warm and dry my clothes. Thankful I was a smoker and took the lighter from my pocket, lit a cigarette, and worked diligently to get the kindling lit until it began burning. Assuming the hail would soon pass, it unfortunately turned to rain and I was forced to remain there for the duration of the night. Alone and wet and cold, I was happy to have found such a place, fearing that my situation could have turned out much worse, a definite drawback of traveling in unknown areas alone. My clothes would eventually dry and I was able to keep the fire burning for the majority of the evening, keeping warm. I would come to treasure this experience and regard it as the best part of my vacation. Early the next morning, I headed up through Vail, nosed around at the sights and beautiful landscape, and decided to take my chances at finding my way back to Colorado Springs without using the map. This decision due mostly in part because the night before, I needed to burn it to get the kindling lit. During my last full day with the rental, I quickly made my way back out of the mountains to warmer temperatures, stopping in various towns and taking in various sights. At one point later in the afternoon, I accidentally forgot to check the gasoline gauge and ran out of gas. I was in the middle of nowhere when I dismounted the bike, disgusted with myself for my own irresponsible actions, wondering how the hell I was going to get out of the middle of nowhere, especially since I wasn't even sure what town I was in. Dejected feeling for the first time on the trip, I pulled up a piece of prairie landscape and lit a cigarette while taking off one of my previously many layers of clothes. Suddenly, I looked across the heavily aged roadway and saw a herd of buffalo, grazing in a field about a hundred yards away. Immediately I felt a sense of peace and comfort, and for some odd reason, remembered that motorcycles come equipped with a reserve gasoline tank. Odd how my seeing those buffalo reminded me of reservoir tanks on a motorcycle, I sat there for about an hour, transfixed on the herd, talking with the few passers by who stopped to see if I needed any help, thanking them just the same, saying I was just enjoying the atmosphere. Ironically, it wasn't until I rose for the first time I sat to look at the herd that I checked to see whether or not this bike had in fact come equipped with a reservoir tank, but was relieved nonetheless when I found the switch. About an hour away from my hotel, I pulled off the road to watch the sunset. The violet, crimson, burnt-yellow, and rust colored hues were a sight to behold. Speechless and in awe, I remained motionless until the sun and all of its glory disappeared well into the snow capped mountain sky.

It was my last day there and I intentionally overslept. My plan was to originally wake up early and ride until just after twelve, drop off the motorcycle, pick up the rental car, heading back to my room to shower and pack, then drive myself to the airport for my five o'clock p.m. flight. Upon waking, I quickly dressed and drove directly back to the motorcycle rental shop, feeling as if my experience thus far could not have gotten better, no matter where I would have ridden that day. Once back at the rental shop, I stayed around for about a half an hour, telling the employees of my two plus day adventure, and watched as they listened intently with an almost envious jealousy, wishing they too could have just ridden off into what to them was unknown territories, the majority of the time alone, left to experience their own thoughts and feelings. And on the ride back to both the hotel and subsequently the airport, I would board the plane relaxed and happy at the experience, thankful for how certain things went not as planned, and never wanting to change a thing that happened. Once seated aboard the plane, I quickly fell asleep and dreamt of my vacation alone, excited to take the experience back with me and anxious for the break to be over and get back to work.

CHAPTER FORTY TWO

WITH VACATION NOW officially over, I was driving to work excited to get back to the grind. However, the news that would await both my colleagues and myself upon our arrival, would severely affect the decisions I would come to make about staying in Yarseville High School as a teacher. Fashionably late, as I had more so than not grown accustomed to arriving, while trying to enter the office to sign in, everyone entering the building was directed by the three vice principals to go directly into the auditorium. We were about to have an emergency faculty meeting. Completely unsure as to what this could possibly be about, the staff quickly began whispering and murmuring about what the morning's topic might be. Looking around the room at my co-workers, I noticed Janice and Elsie sitting right next to one another, and upon making eye contact with Janice, I waved. To my shock, she intentionally ignored my greeting, looking down at her hands in her lap as if she were disappointed at something, and maintained her focus on the front of the room. "That's strange", I thought. "Maybe she didn't see me", I wondered. I was then quickly taken from my bewildering daydreaming about Janice's ignoring my greeting and snapped right back into reality by the low, droning sounding voice of our superintendent. Immediately surprised to see Thistle at a meeting this early on the first day back from break, I could only by his attendance surmise that what we were all about to learn would be devastatingly important. At the request of Principal Black, the entire auditorium became silent and Superintendent Thistle began to speak, surrounded by the entire administrative staff from the high school, and various members of the board of education. And as I sat there, anxiously anticipating Thistle's news, I could not believe what I was about to hear.

"I want to thank you all for gathering together here this morning so quickly and I hope everyone had a nice winter break. Unfortunately, due to unforeseen circumstances, the majority of the members you see standing before you have been working just about every day in regards to today's matter at hand."

"What the hell was he talking about?" I couldn't at the time help but wonder. Tossing out scattered thoughts of what it was he was getting at, I stopped myself from guessing and listened on intently.

"As some of you may already know, Gary Pontier has resigned from the district. Now over the next few weeks, possibly months, you are all going to hear various different scenarios of why Mr. Pontier and Yarseville school district parted ways. I want to remind you all that it is strictly forbidden that you talk with the press. I'm sure they will be around the building, waiting outside for staff members to leave, trying to get a comment or opinion about the situation. You are to reply to them saying you have no comment, and nothing else. Anyone found talking to any member of the press, or anyone else for that matter will be dealt with accordingly. As a member of this district, each and every one of you have an obligation to maintain the integrity and well being of this school, therefore, I had better not have any surprises from anyone in this room. Is that understood?" he finally asked, as if we were going to answer him with a reply, afraid of his verbal threats.

His veins were pulsating out of his neck when he spoke and he was sweating profusely. I can't recall what he wore, but his whole outfit and demeanor gave off the impression of being extremely uncomfortable, probably due to the news he was conveying and not his outfit. Not shedding an ounce of light on why it was Gary left, and leaving a sea of employees on the edge of their seats ready to scream out "What happened?" Principal Black immediately stepped in and continued enlightening us on the matter. And it wasn't until then, that I realized that up in the front of the room, along side of Thistle, Black, the three vice principals, and various board members, there stood two uniformed Yarseville police officers, peering out over the crowd with a slight look of disgust, seemingly eyeing up members of the staff, wondering what they knew or were thinking. Much more sincere and disappointed sounding, Principal Black began to speak.

"On Thursday, the last day of school before break, Gary, . . . uh . . . Mr. Pontier was called down to the office by myself, Mr. Thistle, and a number of the board members you see here before you today. Also in attendance were members of the Yarseville police department. Upon being called into the office, Mr. Pontier was told that he has for some time been under investigation for inappropriate conduct unbecoming of a teacher and had a choice to either dispute the charges against him or resign immediately. He opted to resign immediately and therefore is no longer a member of our staff. I'm sure you will hear stories over the next few weeks about what happened, but I am asking you to keep the school's best interests as well as the students' in mind and refrain from talking about it. Having unjustified rumors being spread will only make for a worse situation. We will deal with the situation accordingly and there is no need for alarm."

And before we knew it, we were sent on our merry way to head back to our rooms and teach as if nothing had ever happened, leaving a virtual cornucopia of questions left unanswered about the unforeseen turn of events. Walking out of the auditorium, not a single soul spoke. Too in shock of the news, staff members walked quietly to their rooms to begin what would be the first of many rumored days following the exploits of Gary Pontier.

CHAPTER FORTY THREE

T HE NEXT FEW days of work were surrounded with an aura of secrecy and despair. It seemed as if the staff and students were mourning the death of a teacher. Following standard procedure, I wasn't one to say much, however, I found out early on while working in Yarseville that the less you spoke and the more you listened, the more people talked to you, assuming you were hiding something, trying to pry a bit of news out of you as well. Unfortunately for them, I had nothing to hide, but the theory worked in my favor, just the same. Sure I knew Gary. But I knew nothing about the supposed ongoing investigation. He was the first person in the school I went out with socially to grab a drink. And as much as I appreciated his efforts to organize parties and football pools, making sure that there was something fun to do on a weekly basis, over time I grew to like him less and less. The fact that he told me previously that he forged his grade book and lesson book truly disappointed me. "What the hell was he doing in class, partying and making friends? He had a responsibility to his students and instead he just wanted them to think he was cool", I thought. And the students did love him. He was at every school function, putting in more overtime that his regular hourly work schedule. He was the teacher the kids would go to in order to shirk their responsibilities and get an excuse from if they didn't complete their assignments or were late to a class. Perpetually voted "favorite teacher" by the coinciding year's senior class, along with Doris, who incidentally, counted the votes and as everyone knew had a crush on Gary, was a general fixture in the facility. I had heard numerous times from the ladies working in the attendance office that Gary was forever telling them that I was gay. Not caring much about the opinion of an overweight alcoholic, whose girlfriend was an even bigger drunk and his main goal in life was to be viewed as cool by his students, instead of instilling responsibility and the effects of consequences for their poor choices upon them, therein giving them the skills to learn from their mistakes, I could have cared less about his departure. However, I would come to learn that for a brief amount of time, I was the small majority.

It took about a day or so for the news to quietly get around the building and what was to be the popular version of what happened would turn out to be untrue. The students were talking about how Mr. Pontier was forced to quit because he was so popular and none of the other teachers liked him, ridiculous to think, but touching coming from the minds of innocent children. Staff however began parading around their own versions, some of which were directly from the horse's mouth. Betty Moffit, I would later come to find out, was privy to the information about Gary's dismissal long before we returned from break. Gary had called her and explained that administration was fabricating the whole story; trying to railroad him into quitting because they no longer wanted him in the district. Kate, who had since begun a relationship with Gary's brother Steve, was also in the know of what was going on, due to her spending time with Steve and his family. About two days after the morning meeting wherein Thistle and Black broke the news of our ex-colleagues exploits, Kate and I took a drive to get some coffee during our prep's and she conveyed to me the following story:

It was the Thursday before break and we were all out at the bar. You had since left, and at about eight o'clock, Steve called me and told me that Gary had just gotten fired. Not believing what he just told me, I immediately left and met Gary at his apartment. Already there, Steve answered the door when I knocked and upon entering, saw Mindi and Doris, both trying to console a visibly upset Gary, sitting, head heavy in his hands on the couch. Barely able to speak at the surrealism of the situation, I asked what happened and Doris began telling me that Rachel and Ralph decided they didn't want Gary working there any longer, so they blew a completely innocent situation out of proportion. And as she began to attempt to tell me her version of the story, Gary rose up from between the two and began to give me details.

He said, "On Thursday at about three o'clock, the downstairs lobby was filled with uniformed police officers and members of administration. As I walked towards the office to sign out, I could feel everyone's eyes on me. Once inside the office, Jerry Galler," union president for the high school, "and Shirley Wemple", leading union advocate for the same, "instructed me that their presence was required in the event of my need for representation. Not knowing what any of this was about, I asked them to stay and the three of us were led into the conference room. Once inside, we were met by three uniformed officers, Superintendent Thistle, Assistant Superintendent Dr. Napoleon Ackerman, Principal Black, and Assistant Principals Innocenzi, Masterson, and Walters were all waiting. Scared and nervous because I had no idea of what was going on, I took the seat offered to me by Superintendent Thistle, and was told that I had been under investigation for some time now in regards to inappropriate relations with a male student. They claimed that I had given a student of mine cash at a hotel room here in town and were interviewing students of mine, asking them if anything inappropriate had ever gone on in regards to them being around me. I was then immediately told that I had three minutes to decide as to whether or not I wanted to resign on the spot or they were going to fire me, therein blemishing my teaching record. Shocked from the accusations as they left the room, giving me time to speak with Jerry and Shirley about my options, it was explained to me by these two the extreme severity of the charges, wherein they recommended I resign immediately. Before I could think, the door swung open with a burst of air and I was forced to make a decision. The police had search warrants for my car, my classroom, and my apartment as well. They told me they had already taken the hard drive from my computer and as you can see . . .", pointing over to his desk from where he was standing, ". . . it's gone. I just can't believe they are making these things up."

Interrupting Kate as she finished conveying the meat and potatoes of the story as told to her by Gary, I couldn't help but ask her for her opinion about the situation. Marred by either her new relationship with Gary's brother Steve or just too stupid at the time to see the signs, she said that she believed he was being set up. I couldn't believe her attitude! "He was as guilty as the day is long", I wanted to say, but thought better and remained quiet, therein allowing myself future opportunities to find out more about the situation. Telling her nothing other than I thought it was going to be weird not having Gary around any longer, she thanked me for letting her talk and pleaded with me not to say anything to anyone else about what she had just shared with me. I assured her I wouldn't and we went back into the building to finish the rest of the day.

After hearing the turn of events from Kate, I couldn't believe that someone could be this incredibly gullible as to believing what they were told. Not knowing myself the truth as of yet, I found myself reflecting back on the day I was asked by Gary to watch his class, at that time noticing the disturbing picture of him and a bunch of shirtless seniors, hanging on the wall above his desk. I immediately wished I had rummaged through his desk that day, wondering about the possibilities of what I might have found, assuming that at that time he was already under investigation for wrongdoings. Seeing Rachel in the hallway later that day, she looked as if her dog just died. I asked her if everything was alright and we took a walk back to her office to have a brief talk.

"I just can't believe this happened. It's just so horrible. I feel responsible as if I should have known. Thinking back, I guess there were signs."

And with that confirmation from my supervisor that I was not the only sane-minded individual who wasn't going to believe this pedophile's bullshit, I began doing a little investigating of my own.

CHAPTER FORTY FOUR

T HE NEXT FEW days were filled with rampant whispers from students of how Mr. Pontier was screwed out of his job because he was such a great teacher. Staff was for the most part split down the middle, the majority of the older staff members, save Betty who was visibly upset by the whole situation and unsure of what to think, and Doris, who to this day will go to her grave believing Gary to be innocent, already believed him to be guilty and were happy to have seen him go. Thinking back, I'm still disappointed at how their opinions were formed based on his being too social and they feeling left out of his invites to various planned after school events, as opposed to his complete and total disregard for the safety and well being of his students.

Making my way downstairs to retrieve my mail at the end of the day, I ran into Don Forman, security guard and ex-Yarseville township police officer. Don had an ear for gossip and an affinity for spreading it to anyone who would listen, prefacing most things with, "Now don't tell anyone else, but, from what I heard . . ." knowing damn well you were not the first person he was telling, nor would you be the last. Grabbing me on my way out and back up to my room, he asked me to take a walk. Up the stairs and back into my room, I politely asked Corbin to step out for a moment, allowing me some privacy to speak with Don. Once Corbin was outside and the door closed behind him, Don suggested we sit and he began telling me everything he knew.

"Your buddy . . .", as he jokingly liked to refer to Gary when speaking to me, ". . . is in some deep shit. He's got himself in a world of trouble with little if any chance of escape. And from what I hear they're finding, he may go away for a long time."

Don always liked to preface any gossip he possessed with a long drawn out beginning, assuming that he was building the suspense of what was unfortunately more so than not, a crappy piece of news. However, this would not be the case today.

"Guess what my buddies found when they searched his car?" he asked coyly, in am almost playful manner, resembling a small child with a secret.

Frustrated at his annoying means of getting to the point, I blurted out, "Your head on a stick? I don't know man, just fucking tell me already!" Smiling at how he at this point had me sitting on the edge of my seat, hanging on to his every word, he continued.

"A box."

"That's it?" I said angrily, wanting to hop across the desk at my impatience with him to tell me something of meaning in regards to the situation.

"So are you gonna tell me what was in it?" I asked, barely refraining from, at this point, wanting to beat the answer out of him, when he finally unleashed what Mr. Pontier's inappropriate behavior was really all about.

"When my buddies down at the station searched Gary's car they found a box filled with pictures of male students of his. Some from the past and some he's teaching this year, and a lot of them were of guys with their shirts off. There was one in particular of a kid, I'm not sure of who it was, sitting in a chair in his classroom, hands tied behind his back with a blindfold on, wearing no shirt. And that's not all. They found a notebook along with all the pictures in the box referring to specific students where he wrote graphic descriptions about their bodies and what he wanted to do to them sexually. My buddies down at the precinct tell me he's fucked. They also took the hard drive from his computer and found that he'd been accessing gay child pornography sites. Oh yeah, and in the box they also found a leather whip and ball gag."

Stunned and speechless at what I was hearing, Don continued.

"The boys down town are interviewing a number of students, asking them lots of questions about Gary and how he was as a teacher, trying to find out if they know of any other instances where he did things wrong. I also heard that he took some kid to a hotel room a couple miles from here and paid him three hundred dollars. Wonder what that was about? They also claim that on numerous occasions Pontier would take that same male student out to the football concession stands after school and engage in inappropriate sexual behavior."

And just then it hit me. That's why Gary had been late as well as absent from so many of this year's social functions. He wasn't studying for his last semester of classes; he was being an irresponsible scum bag, preying on the minds as well as the bodies of his young male students. Don would finish telling me what he knew with an unverified report of Pontier having small groups of male students over at his apartment on weekends, providing them with beer and watching Brittney Spears videos, telling them all to take off their shoes and shirts and get comfortable, saying how hot Spears was, actively portraying the part of a beer swilling cool older guy who really dug chicks, when in reality, he was engaged in his own perverse agenda.

Once Don left, Corbin reentered the room, asking me if everything was alright, noticeably concerned by the strange look on my face. Lying, I told him I was fine and went to the bathroom to vomit.

CHAPTER FORTY FIVE

TWO WEEKS HAD passed since the shocking news of Gary Pontier's exploits and the majority of staff and students were rapidly finding out what a pedophilic monster he really was. Surprisingly however, Doris maintained her allegiance to Gary, even posting the one thousand dollars bail he needed to get out of jail upon his formally being charged. Kate on the other hand, caught in the middle having once been very close to Gary and now dating Steve, was about to crack. And I was just the person to help her to do it. Knowing that Don and I spoke and assuming he was keeping me abreast of the investigation, Kate asked me to skip my second period duty and take a ride with her to get coffee. She repeatedly hinted around about wanting to know what I knew about the incident, yet I acted in a manner of omnipotence, as if I knew everything but was unwilling to share.

"I don't like Gary, Kate, and I never really have. I hope they fry his ass and from what I know, he's not getting out of this one. All that bullshit about him calling parents to cover his own ass over the break before we even returned and found out what happened, just so he could look like the caring teacher he tried for so many years to imitate. Getting Doris to post his bail money and trying to convince Betty and you other idiots he's innocent. It's all fucking ridiculous. They have so much shit on him he's gonna wish he never worked here. And you guys who are standing by him, listening to his excuses and lies, even after the union told us to avoid him like the plague. You're all gonna look like asses once the truth comes out. He did some sick fucking shit and so help me if I ever come across his perverted, deceitful ass, he's a fucking dead man!"

That being said, Kate confided in me an incident at Gary's apartment that would forever confirm my suspicions of his guilt. Making me promise never to tell anyone what she was about to say to me, she began:

"You know, I know Rachel and Ralph don't like Gary, but I never fully believed they were capable of making up a story about him so vile in order to get rid of him. And I know that I have been trying to act as if I believed him, but as time goes on and the more things I learn, I'm beginning to think he may be at fault. One day about two months ago, right around the time his brother Steve and I started seeing each other, we went over to Gary's and were waiting for Mindi to arrive so we could all go out to dinner. While waiting for Mindi, Gary decided to take a shower and get ready and Steve was on the phone with a client from work, leaving me in the living room by myself. Bored and alone at the moment, I decided to turn on the television and wait for everyone else to get ready to leave. Looking around for the remote, upon seeing it, I reached over the arm of the couch to pick it up and knocked over a picture of Gary and Mindi, sending it sprawling out onto the floor and dislodging the picture and its back from the frame.

When I reached down to pick up the pieces, initially relieved I hadn't broken the glass, I noticed that there was a picture hidden behind the one of Gary and Mindi. When I put the frame and picture aside to view what was hidden, I almost died. It was a photograph of a naked man with a black leather hood on, standing in a room I didn't recognize, with of all things, a black electrical cord wrapped around his testicles while he had a full erection. He also had a black, leather dog collar around his neck, fashioned to a leash he held up over his head, hands tied together in front. Mortified, I quickly reassembled the picture and sat there waiting for Steve to get off the phone."

"You mean to tell me you found S & M porn in that sick fuck's house and you still believed him to be innocent? What are you nuts?! Look, I can understand being supportive for Steve and all, but what about the kids. He had a responsibility to maintain the safety and well-being of his students and he used his position of authority to get his friggin' rocks off! They should string him up and cut off his nuts!"

And with that conversation, Kate never again asked me anything about Gary ever again.

As the year went on, more and more disturbing information came out about the incident, some probably embellished, most of which I chose to believe to be true. The administration worked desperately to keep the entire incident under wraps, attempting to maintain a good image, both publicly and within the school. Appalled as I was for what seemed to be their focus on their image as opposed to that of the well being of the students, I again, as I had with the incident regarding Sandy, become even more disenchanted with the district and school in which I worked.

The following year, Gary was given a suspended sentence of one year, forced to turn in his teaching certificate, never being allowed to work in or apply for a position in education again, and had to register as a convicted sex offender in whatever town he resided. A sentence I felt much too lenient. He never did pay Doris back the thousand dollars she lent him for bail, instead using it to buy an engagement ring for Mindi. This infuriating Doris and lead her to believe that she would never have a chance with Gary. A fact the majority of us already knew. Everyone thought his engagement to Mindi was a farce, using it only to distance himself from the fact that he would be less likely viewed as a convicted pedophile if he was married to a woman. The last I heard, he and Mindi moved to Florida. She took a job as a clerk in a convenience store while he spent his night's bartending at a nationally known amusement park, probably stalking young boys on his days off.

CHAPTER FORTY SIX

WITH THE EFFECTS of Gary's dismissal still lingering throughout the school, the happy hours that followed left much to be desired. The same group of individuals was usually in attendance; however, there was an air of discomfort that would perpetually permeate the setting. It was the end of February and the talk of Gary and his inappropriate behavior was exhausted, therein leaving those in attendance to focus on more pressing bar banter; who was screwing who within our group. Brock was still dating Sue at the time, annoying and manipulative, she would tell him when he could and couldn't join us for drinks. I always assumed he would get sick of her bullshit and eventually for his sake he did. Trixie was dating some local who was just a year out of school, high school that is, and fought with him more than anything else. Bud and Cecelia were still together, but rarely graced us with their presence due to his finishing college and her dedication to cheerleading. J.R. would make a random appearance, talking long and hard about what fictitious girl he "bagged last weekend", of course none of us knowing her, due to the fact she probably lived in the "Niagara Falls area". Tara made her best attempts to attend, usually staying for just one but buying a round for the others in attendance. Betty was no longer around, still affected by the whole incident with Gary; she just didn't have it in her. Mitzy had since found love online and no longer attended, marrying her cyber lover after only three months of dating. Barbara would show up on occasion, but usually only if there was a late night school event later that evening. Kelly and Mike, although not dating, she engaged to the local fire chief in town, remained mainstays, rarely if ever missing. Carla's attendance became sporadic, due to what I can only assume as Kate's relationship with Steve blossoming, even amongst the mist of all the problems with

Gary. I just assumed she didn't feel like being a third wheel, being that she and Kate used to attend together when they were both single. Kate and Steve would still make appearances, thankfully nullifying any discussions about any further developments in Gary's case. Doris spent vast amounts of time with Gary, knowing that it would in the long run affect her job, desperately wanting to plead Gary's innocence, of which no one was interested. And Stacy and Corbin, a recently formed couple were perpetual attendees. I guess things in life truly do change and you can't go back to the way things were. This seemed to be an overlying feeling of the first few happy hours in the weeks that followed. But as time went on, everyone seemed to forget except for Doris of course who made it her mission in life to rescue Gary's, and the happy hour ball was rolling once more.

CHAPTER FORTY SEVEN

IT WAS THE middle of March and things were going as usual, the students and staff all anticipating the arrival of spring break. March is the longest stretch of time one has to work in teaching. It's usually five or six straight weeks without a day off, running sometimes into the second week of April. It was a Wednesday afternoon in mid March and I had just come back two weeks previous from a three and a half day weekend, having to leave a half day on Thursday with pneumonia, but luckily not having to take a sick day the next day to due snow. I was still reeling from the vision of ecstasy that greeted me in the office the week before, she looking for Tom Mathis for what I'd hoped was an interview for a teaching position within the school. At about one thirty in the afternoon, we had a fire drill and were herded out into the parking lot like a bunch of sheep when I noticed Dr. Ackerman talking to a woman dressed in all black. Walking out the door in the midst of a conversation with Margaret Minson about who the hell knows what, I immediately tuned her out and became transfixed on this woman. Stunningly beautiful as she was, and this from only seeing her from the back; I instantly became obsessed with seeing her face. Accidentally and without realizing it, I began to walk away from Margaret while she was in mid sentence and made my way across the small roadway to see this woman's face. As I approached her, I was filled with anxiety and excitement. How do I know this person and who is she? Desperate to see her face, I pretended to approach one of my earlier period students so as to ask him a question and after he and I exchanged a quick unrehearsed conversation about something to do with that day's lesson, I turned to face my future.

There standing before me was the woman who took my breath away just two weeks prior. She looked better than I remember and I immediately realized that I was staring at her but could not look away. Talking with Dr. Ackerman, I watched as he tried to act smooth and debonair, embarrassed for him at his futile attempt as well as how ridiculous he looked standing six inches shorter than her in her four inch heels. It was her, and I would not let her get away again.

Trying to think of a way to interrupt, my lack of any idea of how to do so was stopped by the voice of Pat Masterson, vice principal and behavioral administrator extraordinaire, instructing everyone to return to the building. Unable to speak to her at the time, I would later find out that she was hired by Tom as a Spanish teacher. Another two weeks or so would go by before she and I would again cross paths, but from the day she introduced herself to me in the downstairs teachers' lounge, we began what was to be the start of a long and meaningful relationship together.

CHAPTER FORTY EIGHT

WITH SPRING BREAK now behind us, the first week back to work was hell and Friday couldn't come soon enough. Gathering as usual at the local pub, Corbin, Brock, Mike and I were the first to arrive and would remain there without the others for the majority of the afternoon. Surprised to see Brock allowed out by Sue, we joked with him, prodding him into making fun of Corbin and Stacy, pointing out the fact that he was there without her. Corbin immediately interjected, asking us in an overly serious manner, what we thought of Stacy. "Annoyingly immature as well as quite possibly the most unattractive woman any of us have ever seen", we thought better of sharing our honest opinions about her and decided to spare his feelings. And in not knowing how to respond, we remained silent. Looking dejected in response to our lack of any reply, Corbin went on to say how she wasn't up to par to the level of attractive women he was used to dating, implying that he had gotten "better looking chicks" in the past. The three of us, looking around in wonderment at one another as to what he was getting at, he continued, saying he was ". . . sort of embarrassed but for the time being was at least getting a steady piece of ass." He went on to say that for the time being, he would keep "fucking her" until something better came along. "Something better?" I thought. "Who the hell did he think he was, an Adonis? A hundred pounds overweight, balding in his mid-twenties, and at times emanating a scent other than freshness; he should be thankful someone wanted his dick at all." Listening further, although not believing what I was hearing, nor believing his story that he was ever with anyone much prettier than Stacy, I replied in a manner I felt fitting in order to protect his feelings as well as our friendship. "She's great man, and if she makes you happy, don't worry what anyone else thinks." "You're the poor slob fucking that ugly bitch", I wanted to say but refrained. Agreeably nodding, Mike and Brock condoned my sentiments.

Once off of the topic of Corbin's frightful looking girlfriend, Brock nearly jumped out of his seat, saying that he had dirt. Corruption dirt to be exact, and was dying to share. His words still hanging in the air about the news he was about to convey, I couldn't help but wonder what the hell kind of a district was I employed in. As the story went as conveyed by Brock, Mario Verani, director of maintenance for the district of Yarseville, was in a lot of hot water and would probably be fired by Monday with criminal charges pending. Mario was an older attractive gentleman, for a man, who had salt and peppered hair, a neatly groomed beard, and maintained a good shape for a man of his age. But that was about all anyone could say in favor of the man. A condescending, self-proclaimed know it all, he walked about with an air of supremacy, thinking he was better than everyone else and rudely believing it to be the case. He rarely acknowledged anyone's presence; that is except for his girlfriend Annie Horowitz, one of the high school security guards. She was quiet, reserved, and attractive, an overall nice person in general. I was told by many people that she was "completely nuts" and at times saw her in rare form, but liked her nonetheless. Annie had left her husband, a Yarseville township police officer, about a year ago and started seeing Mario shortly thereafter. Unfortunately for Mario, his wife found out and kicked him out of the house, wherein he moved in with Annie and they'd been living together ever since. I never liked Mario because he walked around as if he were better than everyone. I guess that wasn't the case any longer.

Continuing on, Brock told us that he had been under investigation for the past three years. Mario was found to have been giving no bid contracts for work to be done in the district to his friends. Any job over eighteen thousand dollars was supposed to be bid out to the lowest bid, but Mario was giving jobs to his friends that were up to eighty thousand dollars without bidding them out. Not only that, but he would pad the jobs and take a kickback from the friends he hired. He was also charging the district money for work done on his house, his mother's house, his brother's house, and best of all, Superintendent Thistle's house, who he mentioned was also under investigation by the board of education for things he was yet sure of. Fifteen thousand dollars worth of copper wiring was also unaccounted for at the recently completed elementary school and the cops believed Mario was responsible. And to top it off, Annie was getting fired as well for getting paid to work the last two summers while her boyfriend Mario signed fake time cards for her, in essence paying her for a no show job working security in the school during the summer.

"I wonder how the tax payers and parents of Yarseville would feel about hearing how Mario has been spending their tax money", Brock quipped upon finishing his story. Not knowing how to react or even what to say, I ordered four shots from the bar, looked over at Mike, motioned a cheers to him and said "Here's to being single buddy", and poured the mix of Jack Daniels and Yukon Jack smoothly down my throat, wondering what else could go wrong within this district.

CHAPTER FORTY NINE

I T WAS THE day after I touched her and I couldn't get her out of my mind. Elena Dimania approached me in the downstairs copy room, introduced herself and shook my hand unaware at the time that I was already in love with her. What I didn't know was that from that moment in the copy room on, she too was in love with me. The next few weeks were filled with flirting and carpooling, to and from work. We exchanged numbers early on and began dating and before we knew it, we were a couple. We would spend every lunch together, at first with Corbin and Trixie who had the same period off for lunch as we, and soon thereafter, just the two of us. Still a regular fixture at happy hours, I too was now part of one of the many coworker couples, and was happier than I could have ever imagined. Unfortunately, my happiness seemed to be a problem for the vast majority of my coworkers, colleagues, and worst of all friends and would have to spend the rest of the school year dealing with the ramifications. Thankfully, there were only a couple of months left before summer vacation because the abuse we were forced to deal with was just about unbearable. Rumors were running rampant throughout the school. Teachers I didn't even know were passing judgment on us and administration seemed to be annoyed at our relationship. Both of us young and attractive, me in my mid thirties and her in her early twenties, many people seemed to have a problem with us being together. Elsie Veranski, my ex mentor, had since befriended Janice Brodsky once again, from what I could surmise, because of the fact that Elsie's boyfriend Jerry Galler was up to his neck in union issues, thereby affording Elsie time to again spread gossip with Janice. This rekindled friendship quickly began driving a wedge between Janice and me. I trusted Janice, as I at one time had Elsie, and as the next year came to a close and throughout the duration of my last and final year in the district, I became utterly disgusted with these two women. Having nothing better to do than to make up stories about Elena and I, desperately trying to get us in trouble with administration I quickly grew to hate them both. Thinking back, I still can't believe that two grown women in their late fifties could be so malicious and vindictive. On numerous occasions, they would make up stories about Elena and me behaving inappropriately in front of the students. It was a bold faced lie, to say the least. Responsibly dating, we never acted in an anything but a professional manner in or around work. But this was to be just the beginning of an epic falling out with the two of them that would continue on into the next year, leading me to lose even more faith in the district.

Janice and Elsie's gossip about the two of us was bad enough but I would soon learn that I could not trust anyone except Elena. As the year wound down and Elena and my relationship blossomed to a level of blissful happiness, the people I had once looked to as my friends turned out to be everything but. We eventually began avoiding happy hours altogether, opting to spend our time by ourselves, getting to know each other instead. Frustrated and annoyed that my friends could be so heartless and what I felt was jealous, I would change my views on the majority of them, severing a large number of the relationships. They began giving me a hard time for not hanging out with them as much and for spending the majority of it with Elena. We had gotten to a point where we were rarely if ever seen apart. The hardest of these disappointments was that of Corbin and my relationship. From before the first day he began work, I went out of my way, trying to help him out in his first year of teaching, providing him access to any and all of my lessons, tests, quizzes and overall knowledge. And to pay me back, he decided to team up with his judgmental girlfriend, talking badly about the two of us behind our backs and saying that we made a ridiculous couple, she being so young and me acting as if I were too good to hang out with them any longer. They made judgments without knowing any of the facts, and worst of all, he never defended me as I had numerous times done for him in the past with not only coworkers, but with administration as well. The year ended socially without me really being on speaking terms with anyone from the group except for Mike and Brock and would never again trust anyone as I had Corbin.

CHAPTER FIFTY

THE LAST BIT of disappointing news to hit me that year came with about two months left in the school. Rachel Hayleigh, my respected supervisor and friend, came to me early one afternoon to inform me that she was leaving for another school. Upon her giving me this awful bit of news, I felt the air from within me slowly begin to escape. "How could she leave me? She told me that she loved it here and she could see me fitting in as a permanent fixture with her for my entire career. We were a team. This wasn't supposed to happen. You can't go now!" were all thoughts I immediately had and wanted to say to her. But when I looked into the sincerity of her tired eyes, worn and weary from her ninety minute daily commute each way, her ten plus hour a day schedule, supervising the language arts department in both the high school as well as the middle school, and the after effects of the incident with Gary which were still looming throughout the district, I took pity on her and put my own interests aside. I told her how much she'd done for my career and for me as a teacher and hugged her, wishing her all the success and luck in the world. I would visit Rachel on a more regular basis than usual through the end of the year; knowing that this was to be the last time we would work together and her time as my supervisor was just about over. On the last day of school, we hugged one another and cried, telling each other what a pleasure it had been to not only have been colleagues, but friends as well.

CHAPTER FIFTY ONE

WITH THE LAST day of work just about finished, I sat comfortably at my desk, looking around at possible ideas for how I'd like to rearrange my room for next year, completely unaware that this up and coming year would be my last year teaching in the district. Interrupted from my daydreaming state, Stacy Lipshitz walked into the room, looking for Corbin, and when she saw me sitting there alone, with him nowhere to be found, she froze in her tracks.

"What the hell do you want?" I asked her in a tone of aggravation and disgust.

"Uh . . . nothing, sorry. I was looking . . . ah . . . for . . . ah . . . Corbin", she nervously replied.

"Well if his fat ass were in here, there's no way in hell you'd miss it, so fuck off and get out." And with that, her eyes welling up with tears as if I'd just killed her dog, she dropped her face into her hands and left without saying another word.

About ten minutes later, her knight in shining armor would come to defend her honor, however, Corbin had no idea how much rage had been building up inside me in regards to both he and his girlfriends' attempts to bad mouth Elena and I. Upon his arrival and attempt at being able to confront me on how rudely I'd treated Stacey, the second I saw him enter the room, I let my fury fly.

"Your ugly assed girlfriend was here about ten minutes ago looking for you." I said in a calm, reserved manner without even looking up to acknowledge his presence. "I told her that you weren't around and she could probably find your lumpy butt grazing out on the football field. Better hurry up, 'cause if she gets out there before you, there's no telling what'll be left."

And at that moment, a part of me felt badly about how harsh I was being to Corbin and Stacy, and about how immature it all was. Thinking better of continuing on with this verbal assault, I decided to be the mature one of the two and apologize. But then quickly changed my mind, suddenly feeling that he deserved everything he had coming from me and more.

"Still here?, over emphasizing the sound of the question, raising the tone in my voice as if surprised that he actually was still there. "Don't the two of you have a counseling session at noon? Word is Corbin, your girlfriend fucked one of Tommy Willard's friends". Tommy, an utterly annoying math teacher who liked to run out on his bar tabs and constantly smelled of stale milk and day old cheese, he only got his job as a teacher because his mother worked there in the high school. He only lasted a year, eventually getting transferred to the middle school. Tommy had an eerie way of talking about his mother as if she was everyone's mom. ". . . the first weekend the two of you went out.", now rising from my chair, approaching him slowly so as to keep myself from physically attacking him. "That's right", I continued, "that first night you and Stacy went out with Tommy and his girlfriend then went back to his place. Tommy had one of his friends over from college and the five of you were sitting around drinking late into the evening after going out to dinner. You had one too many, decided to leave, and when you did, that fucking wildebeest you once affectionately referred to as the ugliest girl you'd ever been with but at least she was a steady piece of ass, gave her virginity away to some college band geek she'd just met a few hours earlier. And now the two of you are getting serious. I heard you're even thinking of getting engaged. Might want to consider all that crap you were talking about her that day at the bar with me, Brock, and Mike. They'd make for some really cute wedding vows. And I'm sure she'd love to hear them as well."

Stopping about ten feet away from Corbin, unsure of how he would react and wisely giving myself enough room to get out of the way if he decided to charge me like a rhino, I casually but confidently sat on the edge of one of the front row student desks, anxiously awaiting his reaction.

"Look man", he said in a sad and somber voice, "I don't know anything about Stacy and Tommy's friend Glenn, but as for you and I, I'm really sorry about everything that happened. You don't know how hard it's been for me."

"How hard it's been for you?! I screamed, jumping up from where I was sitting, quickly halving the distance between us. "How the fuck do you think it's been for me and Elena? I find someone great who makes me really happy and you and your bitch assed, whale sized fuck toy decide that the two of you have nothing better to do than mess with it! Did I say anything to you when you started disappearing with that war pig, no longer hanging out at the bar with everyone? And when you did decide to show up and grace everyone with your presence, you were with that Amazon and the two of you were joined at the hip? Did I?", now screaming at him, with only about six inches separating us two. "No! I didn't. And why is that Corbin? Tell me! Why didn't I, huh?! . . . You wanna know why asshole, huh do ya?! Because I thought she made you made you happy, that's why. And for as ugly, two faced, and aesthetically disfigured as I think she is, which, you can now by the way add cheap slut to . . . ," I sarcastically interjected, ". . . I never interfered with your happiness. That's the difference between us dude. You're an ungrateful asshole who no longer has access to his own opinion. You've given your soul away to that horrific looking bitch . . . ," calling her names I would have liked to have said to her face but never having had the chance or at the time and thought better of saying, ". . . and she went and fucked your buddy's friend after knowing him for only a few hours. And you two had a date that same night!" I laughingly said, disgusted at his stupidity. "You've carved a real nice life out for yourself man! Good luck with whatever the fuck that thing is you're dating. Just do me one last favor. I think you owe me at least that for all the things I've done for you this year."

Still surprised as I was that he was just standing there taking my verbal assaults with barely a word or an idea as how to defend his action as well as my accusations, he dejectedly tilted his head to the side, pointing it slightly downwards and looked up at me, as if he were a child being reprimanded by a parent, and replied sincerely, "anything you need". And with that, I asked of him the last favor I would ever ask of my one time friend, colleague and confidant. Looking him directly in the eyes and waiting for him to steadily look back into mine; I calmly and surely spoke the last words I at the time hoped I would ever say to him. "Stay out of my life", and slowly but confidently exited the room, flashing him one last look of disgust and disappointment.

Over the entire summer and the first few months of being back at work the following year, Corbin and I remained on barely speaking terms. We were still sharing a room, but he knew better than to loiter while he wasn't teaching a class there. Apparently the news of Stacy having sex with some other guy the first night they went out was news to him and for a brief period of time, put a great strain on their relationship. I wouldn't say that this made me happy, but as the saying goes, what comes around goes around, and I could not help reveling in their feelings of misery. They would eventually get engaged by the end of the next year and by that time, Corbin and I would pass each other without so much as a word. He tried on various occasions, seeming genuinely sincere, to apologize and tell me that we were like brothers at one time. Crying and following me around the room one day after school, he begged me to forgive him for being such an asshole, wherein I slowly turned, grabbed his face by the sides in a sincere and loving manner, looked deep into his eyes, and kissed him smack on the lips, saying only "I knew it was you Fredo", mimicking a scene from the Godfather movie, and walked away, refusing ever again to speak to this man for as long as I lived.

CHAPTER FIFTY TWO

S UMMER HAD FINALLY arrived and the world wind romance I had begun with Elena just four months prior was blossoming at a rapid rate. We spent what seemed like every second together, getting to know one another on more intimate levels, me meeting her family and her meeting mine, thoroughly enjoying every passing second with this woman who was now the center of my life. We would take long walks in the park, go out for rose pedal flavored ice cream or almond milk, listen to live jazz music in the city, while she drank margaritas and I sipped twelve year old scotch. We viewed museum exhibits, attended art gallery openings and had lunches at quaint little hideaway places in the middle of nowhere. We took day trips that seemed to last longer and longer into the night, eventually spending our nights together, sneaking off to some motel along the highway, passionately intertwining our flesh, exploring one another's bodies so as to try and become one. I loved this woman with all that I was and was grateful for the opportunity to not only have met her but for the chance to have loved her. I felt as if I could not be without her and she would eventually become the deciding factor when offered an opportunity of a lifetime.

About halfway through the summer, I decided to go up to Yarseville and set up my room. Elena's grandmother was visiting from Miami, and I had the day to myself. I loaded up my recently purchased truck with every stitch of teaching material I had, and made my way back to the town I at a time once loved. Arriving early in the day at the end of July, I assumed I would be free of running into anyone I worked with, and about ten minutes away from my destination, the thought dawned on me that I may not even be able to get into the building. Relieved as I was upon gaining access through the main doors at the front of the school, I went inside empty handed to see if I could get into my room. Not having the key and again feeling as if I should have better thought out going there so early in the summer to organize my room, I luckily ran into Don Forman, ex Yarseville cop and school security guard who was working that summer for the poor sap who replaced Mario at the end of last year, after his termination.

"Hey stranger", Don said surprisingly, looking at me as if I were lost. "What the hell are you doing up here this time of year?" Quickly realizing that it was "down here" from the direction which I'd traveled from, I thought better of saying anything, thereby confusing Don, saying instead, "I figured I'd beat the end of the summer rush and set up my room early. Plus I don't feel like dealing with that fat bastard when he comes in. He'll have to live with things the way I want them", referring of course to Corbin.

"Still not talking to Corbin, huh?" Don asked, questioning me as if something had changed since the last day of school.

"Why the hell should I? He's a moron and he's no longer in possession of his own decision making skills, or his balls for that matter. His girlfriend runs his life and I can't stomach the sight of her. Plus with all the shit they talked about Elena and me, I just can't forgive that." Continuing on, I remembered what had happened just the week before. "Elena is so pissed at her that she hired an attorney and is seriously considering suing Stacy for defamation of character. She called her up about a week ago and verbally tore into her, telling her all about the lawyer she hired and what she was going to do to her if she ever talked about her again. You should have heard it! Stacy was studderin' like an ass, all nervous and jerky, apologizing to Elena profusely, saying she never said anything bad about her. It was great! And not long after Elena hung up with Stacy, leaving her in a state of confusion and fear, the phone calls started coming in to me. Kate, Trixie, Doris, and Kelly, all called me within the next twenty four hours; the four of them nervous that their immature attempts at badmouthing the two of us now had possible legal ramifications. When Kelly called, kissing my ass of course and trying to find out whether or not her neck was in a noose with us as well, which, of course it was, asking me how Elena and I were doing, as if she really gave a crap, she conveyed to me that yesterday afternoon, Corbin called her and said that Stacy had to be rushed to the hospital with severe anxiety. "Sucks for her, eh dude?"

"You're one crazy son of a bitch man.", he said, after hearing how Elena and I were torturing our coworkers during their summer vacations.

"Serves 'em right, who the fuck are they to pass judgment on the two of us? Just because they're all living out a miserable existence in their own shallow sheltered lives; doesn't give them the right to talk about us."

"Remind me never to piss you off.", Don said laughingly, and proceeded walking with me to the room. On the brief walk there, he told me that three more teachers quit last month, bringing the number of people leaving the high school alone to thirty-eight. Knowing that Don had been working in the district for quite a few years now, I asked him if he knew how many people left in the last three years.

"Close to a hundred I think. Nobody tends to stay around this place for very long. But hell, can you blame them?"

We arrived at my room a moment later, he unlocked the door with me thanking him, and we parted ways until the first day of school. I spent the majority of the day setting things up my way, purposely sending the message to Corbin upon his arrival at the end of summer that he was working in my room, the whole time hoping he was one of the three people Don previously mentioned.

CHAPTER FIFTY THREE

I T WAS THE first non-weekend day in August and the sun was shining bright after what I remember to be about five straight days of rain. I was sleeping in late, missing the early morning warmth of the still rising sun, and still reeling from my date the night before with Elena, when the phone rang, jarring me from my previously undisturbed slumber. Initially answering it, I recognized the voice on the other end of the phone as familiar, but due to the fact that I was just seconds ago fast asleep, couldn't recognize who possessed.

"Did I wake you?" the voice politely asked after having first said my name to no reply.

"Yes, I mean no, this is Jared; you didn't wake me. Who's this?" I groggily inquired, trying desperately to figure out who was calling.

"It's Rachel Hayfield from Yarseville! How are you, sweetie?" she quipped with fervor and delight resounding in her voice.

"I'm great . . . how are you?", mustering the words through a long, drawn out stretch, still lying beneath the covers of my bed.

"Wonderful! Just wonderful! Listen, I know how much you love working in Yarseville and you're well on your way to getting tenure there, but the most amazing opportunity just arose and you were the first person I called. A vacancy in the English department just opened up here at Central Regional . . ." the school Rachel left Yarseville for, . . and I immediately told the principal about you. We were wondering if you were available to come in for an interview." Still surprised and unawake as of yet, I sat up still unsure of whether or not I was dreaming and said, "Wow . . . that's great . . . sure . . . when?"

"How about today?" she excitedly asked back immediately.

Assuming Elena would understand the opportunity, as well as the fact I would have to push our early afternoon date to the Museum of Modern Art back a couple of hours, I said, "Sounds perfect", and we quickly set up a time and exact meeting place.

The drive over was somewhat hectic, with road construction being done for miles on end, wondering to myself that if I took the position if offered to me, would the commute be this dreadful. Happy and relieved that Elena encouraged me to go, telling me we could go out next week and she would instead come over and cook me dinner at my place, I was in a great mood. I arrived about fifteen minutes early, thankfully having given myself enough time to arrive so as not to embarrass Rachel with tardiness, I made my way inside the building and was taken to Rachel's office by a polite mannered secretary lurking about in the main office. Embracing me with a warm hug and kiss on the cheek upon seeing me, both of which I sincerely returned, Rachel formally introduced me to the secretary who brought me to her office and she began telling me all about her new job. Although it hadn't officially started with students, Rachel had been working diligently all summer long, trying to tie up loose ends in Yarseville while preparing herself for her initial year at Central Regional. We spoke for a bit, catching up on life over the last month and a half of not seeing each other, and I thought better discussing my rapidly growing frustration within the district she so wisely chose to leave. We then took a tour of the enormous sized buildings. She pointed out how technologically advance the district was in comparison to Yarseville, and we eventually made our way to meet the principal.

A tall Caucasian woman with short blonde hair and an aura of unchallenged authority, she spoke in the politest of manners with an advanced vocabulary, keeping me on my toes during the entire interview process. A lovely woman to have spoken with in general, before I knew it, she jokingly said after just a few brief questions, that she was thrilled beyond description to have Rachel on her staff. She continued on saying that I came highly recommended by Rachel, motioning to her with a nod of her head and a raise of her eyebrows as if to have her agree that this had been the case, and that this Q & A session was more of a formality and although I probably had a host of questions for her, she would like to offer me the position. "Excuse me?" I surprisingly said, thinking I had misheard her offer. She then laughingly told me that Rachel wanted me here and what Rachel wants, Rachel gets. Impressed but not surprised by Rachel's ability to be trusted with such magnanimous decisions so early on in her career there, I genuinely thanked her for the offer and asked if I could have a few days to consider it. Smiling, she rose from the seat behind her desk where the early afternoon sun shone in through the windows behind her, casting long shadows across the room and making her appear taller than she actually was, extended her hand to shake mine wherein I did, and told me that it was a pleasure meeting me and she hoped I would seriously consider the opportunity.

Walking out towards the parking lot, I felt as if I could have conquered the world. Excited at the prospect of working for Rachel again, we hugged once more, this time good bye, and I excitedly told her that I would call her with my decision in a few days. That phone call, to my dismay, would be the last time I ever spoke to Rachel, even to this day.

CHAPTER FIFTY FOUR

M Y DECISION TO not take the position at Central Regional was a difficult one. I remember on the drive home from the interview feeling a sense of accomplishment and prestige. My supervisor left for another position and arranged to have me go and work with her. "Pretty impressive", I thought, and was extremely excited about the opportunity. But after thinking about what starting over again at a new school would entail, it at the time seemed a bit more than I wanted to handle. Not only had I already set up my room for the up and coming year, but I had two years under my belt in Yarseville and was about to begin my last year before tenure. Vast amounts of staff members were fleeing for greener pastures and I was on the fast track to seniority in my department. I loved my students and their parents as well, and was a main fixture at every single extra-curricular event the school had to offer. I felt that by leaving at that juncture in my career, I would be letting too many people down; all of whom I felt was counting on me. I couldn't just abandon them. Plus, I really loved working there. Even with all the ridiculous nonsense I was forced to put up with that last year. I still loved going to work every day. And I have to admit that working along with Elena weighed heavy on my decision making process as well. We were just starting out in our relationship and everyone who we once thought to be our friends were for the most part making our lives at work a living hell. I felt as if I couldn't very well leave her there alone, having to deal with them by herself. I was her prince and I felt that I had a duty to protect the woman I loved.

Weighing my options heavily, deciding what I felt was the best for my career, as well as my personal life in general, I finally decided against leaving and called Rachel to give her the news. She was noticeably disappointed, as was I in having to not only tell her but to miss out on the opportunity to work with her again. Professional and sincere as always, she was very understanding, wishing me all the best in my future endeavors. She told me all about my new supervisor, Andrea Muller, who ironically replaced Rachel at the last job Rachel left to take the position in Yarseville, and now she was coming to Yarseville to replace Rachel upon her departure there. After a few brief seconds of awkward silence, the two of us both realizing that our journeys together would now take different paths; she again wished me luck as I did her and told me to stay in touch. I promised her we would and hung up the phone, feeling dejected at the thought of how I just disappointed my ex-supervisor, mentor, and friend.

The last month of summer was blissful and electrifying. Elena and I spent eternities together, and I would come to know her better than anyone I had ever known in my life. Anxious but excited, we vowed to one another with the end of summer upon us as well as the start of work only days away, that we wouldn't let anyone get to us this year, no matter what they had to say. With this attitude in tow, we headed back to work on the first day, positive and ready to ignore our coworkers' futile attempts at making our lives miserable. Unfortunately at the time, we had no idea of what we were in for.

CHAPTER FIFTY FIVE

ASSUMING THE THIRD time would be a charm, the day's first day of work being my third such type of day in Yarseville, I, with girlfriend by my side, entered the auditorium swaggering arrogantly for another session of the "Superintendent Thistle Prophesies", as well as the seemingly longer introductions of new staff members by their supervisors, the latter due in part to the fact that every year since I began working there, the turnover of staff members had increased considerably since the first. Once seated, scanning the auditorium for familiar faces, some of which I was happy to see, some of which I wasn't, I noticed Corbin sitting with Stacy. She refused to look over at us as I stared at the two of them with an almost "got something to say now?!" look on my face for what was a longer than usual glance, afraid I guessed at the time to look at Elena cross, fearing a lawsuit being slapped on her. Elsie and Janice were like to little worms squirming in the mud, sitting in the back row off to the left side of the auditorium, whispering God knows what to one another, preparing to eventually and unfortunately interject Principal Black's portion of the meet and greet meeting, incessantly interrupting, so as to seem helpful when in reality, the two only chimed in to hear themselves speak. They were annoying beyond comprehension and their lies and rumors about me would eventually enter into a realm that I was unwilling to tolerate.

Upon Superintendent Thistle's self-assessed venerating speech that damn near put me as well as everyone else in the room to sleep, and Principal Black's reference to the vast sea of new teachers, the supervisors from each department were once again forced to introduce their new cast and crews. It was Vick Walters', vice principal and special education department supervisor, turn to go and upon his introductions of the three new members in his department, one stuck out in my mind more that day than any other. He was the last of the three to be introduced by Vick and upon hearing his name, stood up and actually replied with a "Yo, . . . what's up", accompanied by a wink of his eye, a nod of his head, followed by a smile that even further accentuated his own embarrassing appearance. Wrenching my neck to get a better look at this ludicrous sounding individual, I couldn't help but laugh out loud upon seeing his wardrobe. With gold chain and pinky ring in check, he wore an ashen grey button down dress shirt that was fastened only about halfway up his torso, therein exposing part of his prepubescent hairless chest. His short, black hair was slicked back and shiny, as if held in place with shellac, so as not to disturb a single strand. He sat down before I could see the rest of his attire or come to terms with what I couldn't believe I was seeing. "Did that just happen? I immediately asked Elena amongst a crowd of chuckles and giggles from the attending staff, left in awe at the ridiculousness of his response to being introduced by Vick. "Where the hell did this guy think he was, at a club?" I wondered, still in shock at what I had just witnessed.

Once suppressing my obsession with the half shirtless moron who possessed the grammatical skills of a adolescent, the remaining supervisors introduced their departmental new hires and we disassembled, all heading out to our first departmental meetings of the year. Assuming that this year's meeting would be interesting, seeing as how not only did we have a new supervisor, but six new department members as well, I quickly rushed out to my truck to have a quick cigarette so as to not return late. Once outside, Kelly Sipes annoyingly came running up to greet me, asking how Elena and I were, trying only to find out gossip, and told me she had news, none of which I cared at the time to hear. "You fell in a ditch and that two-faced persona of yours permanently dislodged itself from your personality?" I desperately wanted to say, not wanting to even speak to her and wishing she would leave. "Kate and Steve got engaged last week!" she said excitedly. "Wow . . . that's great.", I replied in an excited, overly exaggerated, even keeled manner trying to convey that if I checked my "Things I Don't Give a Shit About" file, I would find numerous copies. Then raising my eyebrows and looking at her as if to say "are you finished?" I abruptly turned and made my way to my original destination, my final words "Thanks for the news flash!" still hanging in the air.

Back inside the building at our departmental meeting, our new supervisor, Andrea Muller, graciously thanked us all for coming, as if we had an alternative choice, and she nervously introduced herself to the group in a manner not befitting a superior. Attractive and shapely, or so I thought upon initial inspection from a distance but later realized my misperceptions, she was heavily aged for a mother of two in her mid to early forties, especially around the eyes and hands. Her hair was the color of beach sand, speckled throughout with a variety of grey wiry strands. A great set of legs however, I would later come to find out they were attached directly to her head, implying that her head perpetually remained up her ass. She dressed a bit too provocatively for a woman of her age and someone in her position, wearing a short skirt and low cut top not only that first day of work but numerous times thereafter. But for some strange reason, she was able to purvey a slight look of professionalism. She stuttered at times when she spoke throughout the duration of our initial meeting and I remember at the time thinking it was just first day jitters, but would later come to realize that she really had no idea as to what the hell it was that she was doing and was constantly behind in her work. The meeting itself was dragged on for almost two hours, due mostly to the fact that Elsie and Janice took it upon themselves to act as welcoming liaisons for the mew members of the department, constantly commenting with outdated ideas and suggestions to everything Andrea said. Once the two combined century plus old know-it-alls finished with adding their fifteen dollars worth of two cents, we were dismissed to tend to our preparations for the day. Back in the room, Corbin wisely avoided any contact with me, sporadically entering but never staying longer than a moment, only to drop off boxes and put them on his desk, waiting until sometime after I'd left for the day to unpack his things. And Stacy was wise enough to not accompany him on any of his brief trips. The usual cast of characters dropped by at various times to say hello and share their summer experiences, genuinely seeming to care about mine when asking, the whole time finding me sitting behind my desk with no work to do, having since set up the room a month plus earlier and just awaiting my paper work and class lists from administration. I was bored and tired and at times thought of walking around in order to keep myself busy, but enjoyed the fact that my presence made for an uncomfortable inconvenience for Corbin. This was to be my last year at Yarseville High School, and at this juncture I was unaware of it.

CHAPTER FIFTY SIX

THE FIRST FEW weeks of school went off without a hitch. I'd become comfortable as I ever would teaching my classes. My students were having fun, paying attention, and willing to work, and the virtual nightmare of rumors had yet to rise up from the pits of hell from which I assumed they were hiding. Juniors and sophomores I'd taught the last two years were constantly filling my room, coming by to visit or ask for advice with some personal matter, always telling me they missed my class. Elena and I had lunch together every day, alone, just the two of us, and we spoke often about how much we both liked teaching there. My supervisor Andrea and I were getting along infamously; her basically letting me do as I chose, running the entire freshman class how I saw fit; an unforeseen bonus as I saw it. She and I would often speak and although no one could ever replace Rachel, I felt a part of the void of Rachel having left being filled. New teachers in our department were asking me for advice and lesson ideas, saying that they'd heard how much I helped Corbin in his first year. Elena and I began to again attend happy hours, not the warm and friendly environment they at one time were, but made for a way to shake off the dust of that week's work over a few beers with our colleagues nonetheless. She and I were always together and reveled in the fact that the contemptuous crew that at one time felt the need to try and disgrace our good names to both staff and students, maintained an aura of pending fear when in our presence, almost afraid and unsure of how to act around us. Even staff members from other departments were sending new staff members to seek my advice. One in particular was Anthony Vincent Licardello, the scantily clad individual from the special education department, who I initially laughed at during staff introductions at our first day meeting in the auditorium.

Sitting at my desk at the end of the day, waiting for one of the many clubs I was in charge of to convene, there was a knock at my door and in walked Mr. Licardello. Mr. Vincent as I would come to find out he preferred to be called, not only by students but staff as well. A ridiculous sight once again, he began our first conversation with a Brooklyn accented, "Hey, how you doin'? I'm Tony Vincent. Tara said I should come and talk to you. Got a minute?", as he entered the room, approaching me, hand extended, eventually shaking mine upon getting closer. Still sitting at my desk, feet a top and grade book in my lap, reviewing the day's attendance, I motioned to him with my hand, offering him a seat at the desk behind the computer, adjacent to mine. Once seated, he began by thanking me for taking the time to speak with him and told me about how he teaches with Tara, Tara Saltzberg, Spanish teacher who sporadically attended happy hours, buying a round of drinks, would have a quick one of her own, and dashed out the door as quickly as she arrived, three periods of each day. Wondering about his reasons for telling me his daily schedule, I pacified him, looking on intently at him as if I were enthralled in his conversation, patiently waiting for him to get to the point, wherein, he eventually began:

"I'm kinda havin' some problems wit some a duh teechaz downstairs. I keep hearin' dem say stuff about me and how I am when I'm wit duh kidz. An some ah duh girlz ah getting' a little too frienly, if ya know wat' I mean?, he said, laughing and smirking as if he were trying to impress me by the fact that high school girls found him cute, leaving me in a state of anger, not only by his thick Brooklyn accent, that I would later come to find out he had somehow perfected living in Jersey, but also by how he told me what it was he was telling me. Barely able to listen to his accent any further, I interrupted, first telling him to ignore the staff's comments about him.

"There's nothing you can do to stop it and they're just bored and frustrated with their own miserable lives. They have nothing better to do than talk shit about new teachers. You're not the first and you won't be the last. They're just jealous that you have a good rapport with the kids. Don't let them get to you because it's not gonna stop, believe me, I know. As for how you are with the kids, I have one piece of very important advice to give you so listen up." That being said, Tony inched himself to the edge of his chair, elbows on his knees, hands clasped together in front of him, transfixed on what I was about to say and I continued.

"It doesn't matter what you do or don't do, it's how others perceive what you are doing. Now you're maintaining a professional attitude when dealing with your students, especially the girls, right?" I asked him, in a manner sure that he would say yes, yet partially unsure as to his pending answer due to how he first told me about them being overly friendly with him, wherein he did.

"Just make sure that no matter how appropriate you may be acting, no one can mistakenly perceive your actions as inappropriate, got it? These students are very young and impressionable. They see a young, attractive teacher like you and quickly develop a crush on their teacher. They flirt, hang around the room after class, and talk about you to their friends in the hall. You need to be aware of all these things and make sure they know that you are an adult and although they may find you adorable, they need to behave accordingly. All the other staff members have to go on is what they see in the halls and hear from the kids. No one is going to come up and ask you what's going on. And if they do, it'll be an administrator made aware of something that may not even be the case. So be very careful about how you act and what you say. Once that stigma is given to you, it's virtually impossible to get rid of it."

And with that, he thanked me for my time and advice, offering to take me out for a beer "one uh dez days after work." With Gary long gone and the gatherings at happy hours now attended by word of mouth alone, I informed him about the weekly Friday happy hours and he said he usually goes into the city on weekends, leaving right after work on Friday's, but would definitely try and make a few. Once gone, I couldn't help but remember how he laughed when telling me that some of his female students were getting a bit too friendly and hoped for their sake, he was not the type of person I would unfortunately find him out to be.

CHAPTER FIFTY SEVEN

I T WAS THE second week in November, and Elena and I had just returned from a four day weekend in Atlantic City, wherein we planned on attending the NJEA Teacher's Conference, but instead opted to gamble, go out to dinner, window shop along the board walk, and spend a majority of our time in the room. Walking into school that Monday morning, I could feel an air of uneasiness but could not put my finger on it, chalking it up to having to return to a full week's worth of work after an extended weekend. The majority of the morning went off without a hitch when Andrea paid me a surprise visit just as I was leaving to go to lunch. She asked me if I had a minute and unsure of her presence, politely asked her to sit as I shut the door. Upon returning and sitting in a seat directly next to hers, she asked me almost apprehensively about Janice and Elsie. "What's the story with Janice and Elsie? They seem as if they really don't like you; Elsie in particular. She apparently went down to Pat Masterson's office, disciplinarian vice principal who was about six feet four inches tall and had yet to crack a smile in my presence for the duration of my employment in the district, and told him that you have been cursing and yelling at the kids in your class and encouraging them to do the same. He in turn called me down to investigate the situation and I told him I would talk to you about it. Frustrated beyond description, I wanted to throw Elsie under a bus! But quickly remembering Andrea was new and had yet to see Elsie in all her stunning glory, I took the next ten or fifteen minutes and gave her a quick biography on my one time mentor and colleague from as much of an unbiased perspective as I could. I told her that I respected Elsie as a teacher and found that the kids really responded to her, but that we had different methods and approaches to teaching. I went on to tell Andrea that I wasn't there to make friends, however the fact that my students got along well with me and I with them, made for a more productive and enjoyable working environment. Elsie, I continued saying, has had a problem with this since I began working here. I went on to tell her about Elsie's relationship with Jerry, how she left me high and dry as my mentor, and how Janice and I would eventually talk about their friendship and possible reasons why Elsie stopped hanging out with her, only to have Janice then chime right in with Elsie and bad mouth me to everyone upon their friendship's rekindling. I find it all to be ridiculous, I went on, telling Andrea that Elsie, as well as Janice, just needs to mind her own business and stay the hell out of mine. I do my job and I don't need her or Janice running a system of checks and balances to see if that's the case.

More angered than before when Andrea first entered the room and gave me this little tidbit of news, I immediately asked her if we could go down and speak with Pat, wherein I planned on clearing my name and setting the record straight. Once there, I thanked Vice Principal Masterson for seeing me on such short notice, informing him that I was teaching my students to the best of my abilities and would not do anything in my class that I wouldn't do if I were getting supervised, pointing out that the past year Rachel had sent numerous college students in to observe my classes. "I must be doing something right" I told him, saying that I didn't appreciate Elsie's mud slinging and could care less about the reason for its occurrence. Finally I told him that I would appreciate it if she was spoken to about her behavior, pointing out that I did not want her juvenile behavior affecting my students and their progress. I repeated my appreciation in regards to Elsie's skills as a teacher, pointing out that we are from different schools of thought. Thanking me for my forthright honesty and for coming directly to him upon having the situation brought to my attention, he flashed me a look of satisfaction, accompanied with a smile. The first I had ever or would ever see come from this man.

CHAPTER FIFTY EIGHT

THE NEXT FEW months became quite uncomfortable for me, working directly across the hall from Elsie. On the surface, she would exude a demeanor as if we were best friends, saying "hi" with a bright and cheery smile, asking me how my weekend was; telling me innocently funny stories about what had happened that day in her classes. Not wanting to be rude but at the same time wanting to push her down a flight of stairs, I usually returned her counterfeit friendly conversation with the same. However, it seemed as if at any available moment, she back to her "old" ways of spreading rumors about fictitious events occurring in my classroom and making up stories about Elena and I being physically affectionate in front of the students. Fed up to the point of no longer being able to deal with her malicious gossip, I decided to seek advice from my union representative. Upon speaking with my union representative, Joan Childress, she told me that she would speak to Elsie if it would make me feel better. Knowing the union's theory about "together we stand, divided we fall", I had faith that Joan would speak to her about us getting along in the best interests of not only our working relationship and the students, but as two members of the same union.

Still fit to be tied, later that afternoon after all the students had been dismissed for the day, I was on my way back to my room from making copies when Elsie came out of her room and asked if she could talk to me. Having as yet to have sorted out my thoughts on the whole situation and being caught completely off guard, I began unleashing a verbal reign of terror down upon that woman that would have lasting effects, unfortunately more so for me than for her. She attempted to touch my shoulder as if to console and talk to me the way a mother does a son, when I reeled back, feigning off her advances, repulsed at the thought of her closeness. Startled, she attempted to spin a web of deceit and lies, telling me that she has never said a bad word about me, upon which, out of the corner of my eye, I saw Joan motioning for me to come into Elsie's room and talk the whole torrid situation out. But it was too late for that. I was already angered beyond the point of return and spoke in a manner to that woman that I would have never thought I possessed. Cutting her off immediately at her telling me how she never said anything about me, I let loose, threatening her to stay the fuck away from me, adding what a miserable old bitch she was who just couldn't mind her own business and had nothing better to do with her life. I continued yelling, now even louder than before, about the pot calling the kettle black when she was making up things about my relationship with Elena when she was married to someone who could care less that she was fucking the goofiest bastard this side of the Mississippi. Pointing down the hall to Janice's room, I next went on about how the two of them were fucking with my well being and my career and said that if something bad were to come from their antics, they would rue the day they met me. I finished off with advising her to "just stay the fuck away from me, leave me alone, and don't ever utter my or Elena's name again, because if I hear that you do, you'll be fucked on levels you never thought imaginable!" And with that, I turned, walking angrily into my room, and slammed the door behind me. Not my finest moment, I must say, but at the time I felt as if she had it coming. I don't so much regret speaking to her in such a manner, but wish I hadn't due to how she would later deal with me verbally assaulting her.

CHAPTER FIFTY NINE

ELENA AND I began attending happy hours on a more sporadic level. Never really wanting to go and rather choosing to spend our time just the two of us, we did so on occasion just to make those staff members who made us at one time feel uncomfortable, feel the same. On one particular Friday late in November, the week before Thanksgiving break, I for some reason found the need to constantly torture Stacy and Corbin, as they sat idly by, forcing them to deal with my stares and comments about how certain people in life are just mean and nasty and what goes around comes around. I even went so far as to mention how when you like someone and you think they like you, but later find out that they fucked a perfect stranger the night of your first date, you get upset and probably later on in life, at some juncture, will do the same to them in return, just to even the score. I continued on saying that even if you are dumb enough to then get engaged to her, referring to Corbin's recently getting engaged to Stacy, it would only be a matter of time before the score was settled. The beauty of this exchange was that they both tried desperately not to let me get the better of them. This forced them to just sit there and take everything I dished out, knowing deep down they deserved it all and more.

To no one's surprise, Tara Saltzberg showed up, buying her customary round for the masses, but stayed for what was to be her story about a fellow coworker of which I wished I'd never heard, yet was expecting to hear for some time. She began telling us about her working relationship with Tony Vincent, and how he was undermining her authority while working in the room with her, letting not only his special education students slide on their work and responsibilities, but was now doing the same with her students as well. She continued saying that she had at that point spoken to him on numerous occasions about the long term effects and ramifications of not holding students responsible for their work and how he should be acting more like their teacher than their friend. What was to come was even more shocking than what she had already conveyed. She told us that as well as maintaining unprofessional teaching practices, of which included fixing students' grades and their attendance sheets, Tony was also acting in a manner completely inappropriate of a teacher. Speaking now so that you could have heard a pin drop to the captivating stares of all the teachers in attendance, I couldn't help but look up at the group and notice that for the first time in what seemed like years, we were all grouped together, forming a sort of bond. She told us about various instances where Tony would sit on the edge of female students' desks, talking about topics completely unrelated to their work at hand, leading them on to believe that he wanted more from them than a teacher/student relationship. He would ask them about where they hung out on the weekends, suggesting that they go and check out places he tended to frequent. He made inappropriate comments on repeated occasions and generally seemed as if he was trying to get to know his female students on a more intimate level.

Floored by Tara's conveyance of events regarding Tony, after a moment of silence, wherein we processed what it was we had just heard, everyone, it seemed had a small little story about him of their own. The first to add an instance of inappropriate behavior about Tony was surprisingly, Stacey, who I assumed at the time did so desperately try and form some type of commonality with Elena and I, for the first time not being on the attacking end of our discussions. She mentioned how one day she saw Tony standing in the hall, shirt unbuttoned down to the middle of his chest, as was his usual statement of fashion, talking to a female junior. She was standing in the hallway with her back up against the locker while Tony stood just inches away from her, right hand on his hip and left hand up over her head to the side, supporting his predatory stance. She said she didn't know what they were talking about, but he looked as if he were trying to get her phone number.

The next story came from Brock. He said that last Tuesday, he had to run out to the parking lot to move his truck around to the back of the building to load some audio visual supplies for that nights board meeting, when he saw Tony leaving, shouting "yo's" and "was' up's" to girls calling out his name upon their departure. The whole time unbuttoning and removing his dress shirt, therein revealing a skin tight, white tank top, as he unprofessionally made his way out to his low end model Cadillac. Brock continued that as he backed out from his space and sped off through the sea of departing students, Tony responded to their calls of "Bye Mr. Vincent", with howls of "See ya beautiful" and "Hey sexy".

Kelly Sipes, always one for adding to the gossip, interjected, telling the group how she has to work with him for one period of the day and she constantly has to tell him to stop talking to the students while she teaches, the majority of who are females. He constantly undermines her authority by trying to make excuses for the girls in class when they don't come prepared, saying that he'll talk to me and take care of it.

Eventually having heard enough, now sick to my stomach at the thought of working in the same building with this person, I asked Tara if she had said anything to his supervisor Vick. Somewhat surprised at the idea, she said, "No, do you think I should?", wherein we all replied with a host of affirmative responses. Tara's story of Tony's antics, somehow brought us all together that day, and I remember feeling happy about again experiencing things the way they once were.

CHAPTER SIXTY

MAURY SAUDERBERG, PERPETUAL pessimist and self-proclaimed pervert, was a long time English teacher at Yarseville Battle Monument High School. He hated teaching his classes, especially the kids, and constantly complained about everything in a high pitched, whiny voice that grated on the nerves of anyone in listening distance. Maury taught low level reading and could be found on more occasions than not, sitting behind his desk reading the day's newspaper, while his students sat around idly chatting. And during his prep and lunch, Maury would, to the protests of his colleagues, take off his shoes and stretch out on the dilapidated sofa in the teachers lounge, sleeping so soundly that at times he would actually snore. Irresponsible and lazy to the point of every so often having to check him for a pulse to see if he was still alive, Maury was to be the next Yarseville employee involved in a scandal at the high school.

It was about ten thirty in the morning, about two weeks before winter vacation. The students were restless and tensions were high among teachers; all of whom were anxiously anticipating the arrival of our break. Kate Michaels, recently engaged to Gary's brother Steve, was downstairs in the main office spreading holiday cheer and telling anyone who would listen about how happy she was about her future wedding plans, of which they would take up the majority of her class time wherein she was supposed to be teaching, when Principal Black entered from his office and asked her if she was teaching a class at the moment. Surprised as she was, assuming that her presence in the office gave credence to the belief that odds were, she wasn't teaching a class at that time, she replied, "No Ralph, did you need me for something?", smiling, with that perpetual deer in the headlights look she would assumingly maintain throughout her engagement. "I need you to go up to your room and cover Maury Sauderberg's class right away.", he succinctly said, opening the door leading out into the hallway for Kate to immediately proceed upstairs. Following her out, he stopped just a few feet away, motioning to her with a nod of his head to continue directly on, while he began speaking to two uniformed Yarseville police officers.

Once in the room, she immediately noticed Maury's absence and instinctively, noticing the class was, up until her arrival, unsupervised, asked the class as a whole about his whereabouts.

"Mr. Masterson and a police officer came up and got him about ten minutes ago, but I'm not sure where they went." replied a small, freckle faced freshman with glasses and blonde hair. "Is he gonna get fired?" the young boy continued, asking in a manner not reflecting the seriousness of a situation in which someone could possibly lose their job. Unsure at to what had recently gone on since her departure from the room just one period prior, her curiosity immediately got the better of her and she found herself saying, "Why, what happened?!" And right before the innocent looking student could reply, Elsie stuck her head in the door, her face adorned with a look of content, and asked Kate if she had heard what happened. Not knowing but desperately wanting to find out, she excused herself for a moment and stepped out into the hall to get the juicy news from Elsie.

Once out in the hall, Elsie excitedly began telling Kate that at the beginning of the period, Maury arrived late to class as usual, and his students were scattered about talking to one another. He asked them repeatedly to stop talking, but they continued to ignore him. Angry and at a loss with his patience, he walked up behind one of the students in the front row, Elsie being unsure of his name, smacked the student square in the back of the head, hitting him so hard that his glasses flew off of his face and broke upon hitting the floor. The student, obviously shaken and upset, ran out of the room directly down to the office. Within ten minutes, he was downstairs in the office with the police. She finished saying that she heard he was getting fired.

As the day went on, rumors were spread as to the severity of the actual situation, one actually involving a weapon. The parents of the student involved showed up shortly after the incident occurred, mortified and wanting justice for Maury's inappropriate actions. So a behind the doors deal was made, wherein staff and any students that asked were told that Mr. Sauderberg was taking early retirement due to unforeseen health problems, when in reality, he was fired, but still able to collect his pension. And once again, Yarseville Battle Monument High School maintained its counterfeit integrity by covering up yet another scandal within the district.

CHAPTER SIXTY ONE

HAVING BEEN BACK from winter break for about a month and a half, mid-term exams were over, the students were already talking about spring break, which was still about month and a half away, and Elsie was still basking in the afterglow of Maury Sauderberg's dismissal, again spending the majority of her time at work gossiping with Janice while the two spread rumors about everyone and anyone they could think of. Kate Michaels had apparently lost a lot of weight when I initially met her, due mostly to the divorce with her first husband she was going through at the time. Now happily in love and engaged to Steve, she began putting the majority of the weight back on. Noticing this, as it was hard not to, Elsie concocted a story that Kate was pregnant, going so far as to apparently have told people that it wasn't even Steve's. She also continually embellished the incident with Maury whenever anyone asked her about it, constantly wanting to discuss it, as if she had a hand in his dismissal. Elsie was a frustrated and miserable old woman who could never mind her own business. She never looked at things in a manner in which they could affect someone's livelihood, and it was directly because of her that I began my falling out with my supervisor Andrea Muller.

Up until that point, I was viewed by administration as well as my previous and current supervisor as an asset to the English department. I had since written the curriculum for all three levels of freshman English as well as the mid terms and final exams, organized and brought before the board to be sanctioned, two clubs, started from the ground up, volunteered for every extra curricular, after school event, and had not a single blemish on my record. My observations, nine in all over my three years in Yarseville, were exemplary, and I was already offered tenure and signed my contract for the next school year. Elsie and Janice had since seemed to be focusing their fabricated banter on other staff members, relieving me and leaving me to stay focused on my work, when one about a week before spring break, Andrea stopped by my room in the middle of one of my morning classes and asked me to stop by her office and see her immediately following the lesson. Surprised at the time, wondering what could be so urgently pressing, I couldn't help but wonder at the time what it was she needed. Making my way to Andrea's office, nothing would have prepared me for what I was about to experience.

Sitting behind her desk, surrounded by various mounds of unfinished paperwork, I knocked on the door to the highly air conditioned room, wherein looking up upon hearing the knock, she motioned for me to come in.

"Have a seat", she said, in a voice unbecoming of her usual pleasant demeanor. "We need to talk", she then said, instilling in me a sort of nervousness I had never before experienced when speaking with her. Having asked me to meet her in her office on various occasions since, on the brief walk to her office from my room, I had assumed that day would have been no different than the rest. Unfortunately for me, I was terribly wrong. Seated and wondering why her attitude and demeanor towards me exuded condescension and negativity, I sat for the next twenty or so minutes defending myself against accusations I never thought imaginable. She began by telling me how she felt my work as of late was questionable, asking me to justify not only lessons I had taught, but about my methods teaching them. Flabbergasted and in awe of her accusations, I immediately defended each and every one of her concerns, repeatedly asking her why all of a sudden she was having issues with my work when up until that point she seemed more than fine with my performance. Talking back and forth and getting nowhere, I couldn't understand where her change in attitude had come from. Frustrated, I told her that I wasn't going to change my methods, wherein she informed me that there would be consequences I would not appreciate. Getting up from the chair, I gave her a look of disappointment and said, "We'll see about that.", and left, never again trusting her as long as I lived.

CHAPTER SIXTY TWO

WE HAD BEEN back from spring break for about a month and the end of the year couldn't arrive fast enough. Andrea was continually complaining about me, saying she was not happy with my work. She would drop by on numerous occasions to supervise me unannounced, and unfortunately for me she was well within her rights, having not yet gotten to my first day of my fourth year wherein I would receive tenure. However, I was lucky enough to have already have had my official observations completed. Janice and Elsie were walking around with their heads held high, basking in the glow of the aftermath of my falling out with Andrea and I was rapidly approaching my limit as to what I could further handle. Unsure of what to do, I decided to go and see Principal Black, and it was a decision I did not make easily. I am not one to be a burden to others and felt as if the whole situation was juvenile and embarrassing, therefore felt almost ridiculous going to Ralph about it. Plus, just off the heels of Maury Sauderberg's dismissal as well as Gary Pontier's suspended sentence making hushed news around the district only a week before, Ralph was dealing with the constant complaints from numerous staff members about continuously inappropriate behavior regarding female students by Anthony Vincent. Although Ralph, as well as the other three administrators was informed by various staff members, they seemed to be altogether ignoring Tony's inappropriate behavior. I began to feel as if my professional world was falling apart and I rapidly began approaching the point of not being able to work under such strenuous conditions. So with much self deliberation, I decided to go and speak with Ralph.

Sitting in the main office waiting to see if he had a moment to speak with me, I felt uneasy as well as nervous, unsure exactly as to what it was I was exactly going to say to the man, and upon entering his office, I let go of all my emotions, allowing them to get the better of me and once behind his closed door, I began to cry. By this point, I had become an emotional wreck, feeling as if everyone were out to get me. All I ever wanted to do was to teach my students as best I knew how and live my life analogously. Never in my wildest dreams would I ever think that things would have gotten so bad and out of control. Unfortunately for me, they had, and before I knew it, I found myself in hysterics, telling Ralph I wanted to resign.

Thankfully, or so I thought at the time, he calmed me down, helping me put things into perspective, and told me that it didn't matter what anyone else thought or said. What mattered was that what I was doing was in the best interests of the students and he was fine with that. We continued talking for a good half an hour and I told him all about my relationship with Elena and how it affected our relationship with a number of fellow staff members. I went on to explain how Janice and Elsie were constantly spreading rumors about me and that they were affecting not only me but my students as well. And lastly I informed him about Andrea's change in attitude towards me and how she, without warning or provocation, began supervising me unannounced, telling me at every chance she got how she felt my work had become substandard. Then with a pat on the back and a look of reassurance, he told me to keep on believing in myself and doing what I was doing for the sake of my students, saying that he would speak to Andrea and have the whole situation taken care of. Thanking him, I for the first time in months I felt relieved, as if everything was going to be alright. Little did I know, I was on the heels of the end of my career as a teacher in Yarseville.

CHAPTER SIXTY THREE

HAVING GONE TO speak to Ralph, I initially thought that this was a good idea, and not being one to jump ahead in order when it comes to the chain of command, after talking with Andrea and getting nowhere, I professionally took what I felt at the time to be the appropriate next step, and went to her supervisor. This unfortunately, did not go over well with her and would be an irreparable event that Andrea and I could not get past. Over the next two weeks, she maintained virtually no contact with me at all and I initially thought everything was going to be alright. That was until Ralph called me down to the office and told me that Andrea was rescinding her recommendation for my tenure. Disappointed at yet another setback in my professional career wherein other individuals were trying to make my life miserable, I was not surprised by her behavior, but wrongly assumed that Ralph would tell me how he would support me. It was the least I felt he could do, seeing as how all I had done for the school and my students, and had no other reason to think otherwise. It made sense to me being that I had never been called down by administration to be spoken to for any reason whatsoever except to thank me for either volunteering to help out with extra curricular activities or for exceptional work. I rarely if ever sent disciplinary problem students to the office and not only turned in paperwork on time, but early on almost every occasion, usually to the dismay and aggravation of my constituents who themselves would be lucky to turn things in on time. My record was completely unblemished and my observations near perfect with lists of commendations and literally no recommendations. The thought of Ralph actually not supporting me came as an unforeseen surprise, to say the least. Sitting me down in his office, he explained to me that Andrea had already spoken to a member of the board about having my tenure offer revoked and further explained that even though I had been offered a contract for next year, if I chose not to resign, she was going to request a hearing before the board of education members, reconsidering my recommendation for reemployment, wherein I would be forced to defend myself and possibly face termination in the event I were to lose. I couldn't figure out why she was being so vindictive and malicious. This woman was disrupting my livelihood and apparently felt no remorse about tentatively ruining my professional career. I would however, come to find out not only the reason for her malice and cruelty, but a bit more than I bargained for as well.

CHAPTER SIXTY FOUR

I T WAS LATE in May and there were only about four weeks left in school and I was still contemplating what to do in regards to Andrea pushing for me to resign. My initial reaction was to fight the good fight, having Ralph on my side and my untarnished credentials, I couldn't lose. However, for some reason, unknown at the time to me, Ralph was no longer on my side, now not only avoiding me, but asking whether or not I had made a choice in the matter when confronted by him. "How could he have turned around and changed his mind so quickly?" I wondered. Not knowing which choice to make in the matter, I decided to make a phone call to someone who would hopefully give me sound and solid advice.

Nervously, not because I did not know what to say, but about the possibility of his answers, I picked up the phone and began dialing, wherein, he picked up after the second ring.

"Keith? I asked, as the voice on the other end of the phone said hello.

"It's Jared, how are you?" I continued.

"Hey Jared, what's going on? he replied, the tone of his voice sympathetic, as if he knew the reason for my phone call.

"I'm assuming you heard about what is going on with Andrea and me in regards to my getting tenure next year, and being that we have been friends since my start here in Yarseville, I figured I'd get the advice of someone who actually mattered."

"I'm flattered you keep my opinion in such high regard. Actually, your ears must have been ringing. I've been meaning to call you in regards to this whole sordid mess to tell you what I know from my end." "What he knew", I wondered. What could he know? Why would the board president know of my situation already? Was this news already buzzing over at the board office? And before I could ask him any of these questions, he continued.

"You've pissed someone off on high and he's got a hard on to get rid of you?" "Pissed off? Who the hell could I have pissed off, especially someone with authority? What the hell was he saying?" I anxiously wondered. Keith went on to tell me that Dr. Napoleon Ackerman was in agreement with my supervisor Andrea regarding my offer of tenure being rescinded. Immediately wondering what I could have done to aggravate the man, Keith began to tell me a story that would drain every last ounce of faith I had up until that point in the Yarseville school district.

"Here's what I know", he began, reminding me that we never actually had this conversation, as he had in the past during such instances where the two of us would speak about situations involving corruption and unprofessional occurrences. "Not long after your little explosion in the hallway with Elsie in regards to your never wanting her to speak to you again, calling her this, that, and the other, and saying how both she and Janice were infectious to the high school, your one time mentor, Elsie, and her buddy, Janice, decided to go and pay your supervisor a visit. Not only did they give her a list of things you were doing in your room, none of which I want you to know I believe, but also went so far as to say that you have been talking poorly about Andrea, saying what a horrible supervisor she is and talking about her in a less than flattering light."

Speechless at what I was hearing, I was unable to mutter a sound, thereby affording Keith the opportunity to continue on with the news that would set the wheels in motion in regards to my demise.

"Because of this, she has decided not only to make your life miserable, but to get you to quit. And now she has her boyfriend giving her firepower."

"Her boyfriend? What boyfriend?" I asked, not knowing who the hell Keith could have been talking about. "I thought she was married?", I wanted to say, instantly remembering catching her in a more than warm embrace while in the arms of a former male staff member of hers who had come to give us an afternoon in-service on how to get our students to become more productive writers, wherein I overheard the two in the hallway talking about whether or not Andrea had found a new playmate as of yet there in Yarseville, continuing on about how she was still stuck with her "useless, unemployed husband."

"You mean to tell me you don't know?" He said laughingly, as if I had been in the dark about the affair going on right under my nose.

"Who?" I asked him, in an impatient voice, my insides writhing within me at the thought of who could be ruining my career without me having any knowledge of his existence.

"Napoleon", he said, as if I should have been aware of this all along. Still reeling, not only from the news of their affair which was apparently common knowledge to everyone else but me, I immediately realized how it all made sense. Elsie, angered at how I would no longer put up with her gossip and authoritative ways, decided to fabricate stories about me badmouthing Andrea, who in turn, instead of being professional and coming to me with her concerns, took the word of an archaically old gossip syndicate and decided to ruin my career in the district, along with the help of her diminutively sized lover. Still unsure of what to do, especially now in regards to the new information I'd just been exposed to, I asked Keith for his advice. Graciously, he told me that if I wanted to stay, to stick it out and defend myself, wherein he would support me, making it quite difficult for Andrea to get rid of me. However, having Dr. Ackerman on her side, being that he was the assistant superintendent was not going to be easy. But being that I had all positive observations in my file and not a single letter of reprimand, there was a 50/50 chance I would be able to keep my job.

"Why the hell would I want it now?" I asked him. Realizing that even if I did keep it, she would still be my supervisor and I would have to put up with her bullshit for the rest of my career there, writing me bad observations, letting the two dinosaur twins talk crap about me. The whole time knowing that the second I deviated from the norm I was going to have my ass nailed to the wall and get called to the carpet.

"No thanks", I said. "I'd rather shovel shit than work in this district one minute longer." And with that, Keith offered me his condolences telling me to think about it, saying that he would support me in any decision I was going to make.

"Try and not let it get to you. I know it's bad but it's not over 'til its over." he said attempting to reassure me and we hung up.

Dejectedly, I sat there on the front steps to my apartment door, wondering how things had turned out the way they had. I had given everything I had to this school and they repaid me in such a deplorable manner. This was my livelihood, my career, and people found it in their best interests to ruin it. As angry and upset as I was at the time, I think I was mostly disappointed. Disappointed in how my one time friend and boss, Andrea, could use her position of authority to be so malicious and hurtful. Weighing my options to fight the good fight and possibly win, get tenure, and have to work for someone who would spend the majority of her time trying to make my life a living hell, versus losing and having on my record a tenure year dismissal, I decided to turn in my resignation, but not without a glowing letter of recommendation from Andrea as well as Ralph first. Unfortunately for me, that to would be difficult to come by.

CHAPTER SIXTY FIVE

T HE NEXT MORNING, I decided it in my best interest to inform Ralph and Andrea that I would be resigning. Awkwardly, Ralph told me that whatever I needed, he would be there to help me out. "Whatever I needed?" I laughingly thought. "What I needed was for him to grow some balls and stand up for a hard working employee of his who gave every free moment of his time over the last three years to his school!" I angrily wanting to convey. But instead, with hurt and disappointment having replaced my feelings of anger and revenge, I somberly said, "Thanks", and left to go inform Andrea of the same.

Asking her for a letter of recommendation was like pulling teeth. She said that she was extremely busy with her work; or lack thereof I at the time thought to myself, and didn't know when she would have time to write it. Knowing immediately that this was her way of getting out of doing it, I informed her that she would not be receiving my letter of resignation until such time as I received my letter from her and it was to my satisfaction. Apprehensively agreeing with me, I couldn't help but make one last comment before walking out of her office for the last time. "You truly are a professional disappointment and you should be ashamed of yourself. One day Andrea, mark my words, you'll get what's coming to you. You can count on it." That being said, accompanied by a look of disappointment and disgust, I turned and left, wishing as if I had taken the job with Rachel the summer before, therein avoiding this whole sordid experience.

As the last few weeks passed by, the junior and senior proms came and went, both filled with stories of how Anthony Vincent acted inappropriate on numerous occasions, completely oblivious to me while in attendance at both, as I perpetually remained in a state of confusion and despair in regards to my own dismal situation, and I counted the final days left of my career in Yarseville Battle Monument High School. Andrea had yet to give me my letter of recommendation and was still harping on me incessantly for my letter of resignation, therein allowing her to post my vacated position, of which I told her she would not receive it until such time as I received my letter from her. Ralph was now, without emotion, asking me to turn in my letter, wherein I conveyed the same to him in that once I received my letter from my supervisor, he would have my resignation on his desk. Elsie and Janice were more than ecstatic about the news of my departure and out of fear of them again spreading rumors about reasons as to why I was leaving, I decided to inform my students that my leaving the district was a choice of my own wherein I was compelled to do what was best for me at this juncture in my career as well as my life in general. Thankfully, no real rumors that I know of came to fruition about me leaving while again protecting the best interests of my students. I would for the last time put their well being first and against what I'd taught them so many times before, lie, not having the heart to tell them the truth about what a disturbingly cruel place the world can be.

Graduation day had come and it took every ounce of my being to attend with a smile on my face. I actually considered not going and shirking my responsibility, feeling as if the administration had done nothing for me, why should I do something for them? Reconsidering, I decided that up until this point I had remained professional as well as responsible and would not lower myself to my constituents level of immaturity and therefore attended as I was required. Just before the ceremony, while staff was organizing themselves alphabetically and checking on their rows of students for which they were responsible, making sure all graduates were accounted for and seated in the right order alphabetically, I walked to the office to hand in my letter of resignation. I had earlier in the day received my letter of recommendation from Andrea and after having read it, realized it was not worth the paper in which it was written, but realized it was the best I would get. Generalized and impersonal, I couldn't help but wonder how I would get a future job in education knowing that upon anyone checking my references, this woman would make it her mission in life to see to it that I never worked as a teacher again. Wanting to go to Ralph and have him force her to rewrite it, I had grown tired and weary of fighting and just wanted to cut my losses and move on with my life, hopefully teaching somewhere I would be appreciated, doing what it was I so much loved to do. Coupled with the fact that he was now after me to turn in my letter even more so than Andrea, I wondered for a moment what had happened to change his attitude with me, and couldn't help but entertain the possibility that he too was being told by someone, at this point, I could only imagine who, that I was badmouthing him as well. Not wanting to believe this, I kept with the notion that Dr. Ackerman being his boss, he was forced to reinforce his superior's wishes, even if it meant compromising a teacher/administrator and one time friend relationship as well as all but diminish the faith of a soon-to-be former employee about a district he once loved teaching in and at a time long ago and believed in very deeply.

Now out on the football field, seated amongst students, administrators, teachers, parents, children, brothers, sisters, grandparents, aunt, uncles, cousins, friends, neighbors and the like, I couldn't help but wonder what it all meant. This was to be my last graduation ceremony in Yarseville wherein I would be in attendance as an employee. Someone who had a hand in educating the young minds of those seated before me, anxiously awaiting their turn at graduating and going out into the real world and making a difference. Did they really know what it was they were in for? Did any of them know what it all meant? Did any of the unsuspecting attendees know about all of the corruption, inappropriateness, cover-ups and scandals that happened in just the three years I worked in the district? Were they aware how close to home it all was? Were any of them involved already, perhaps unbeknownst to me, or even themselves? Would any of them become future participants in future events that would again require a covering up of a scandal? What did it all mean and why was I so saddened at the finality of it all? And with a heavy heart and a forced look of happiness, I looked around at my surroundings, wishing three years previous I had never interviewed there at all.

CHAPTER SIXTY SIX

WITH GRADUATION NOW a but a fleeting memory and the students having served the sentence of their last day of attendance, my final day as a Yarseville School District employee was upon me. The tearful goodbyes and thank you's from my students, still fresh within my mind, I remained saddened at the reality of it all, and spent the remainder of the morning packing up what little items I had left to take from my room and loaded them into my truck. I purposely spent the day ignoring just about every staff member except for Elena. She could see how hard of a day this was for me and lovingly remained by my side supporting me for the majority of it. At about ten o'clock with only two hours left before I would be rid of this place forever, Elena informed me that she had just been down to see Ralph and resigned her position in the foreign language department, saying that upon telling him, he said he was not surprised to see her. Astonished and in shock at her deciding to leave without yet having another job and not telling me of her intentions, she told me how she was proud of how I handled everything that happened to me, in every aspect and could only imagine what happened to me happening to her in the near future. She continued saying that she no longer wanted to be a part of a district that put more emphasis on gossip and covering up scandals than they did on the education and safety and well being of its students. She felt it was morally reprehensible and she would sooner have no job than work another minute in that district. Telling me this, the entire time giving me a look as if to say that it was ok that I was leaving, she too wanted to be a part of it as well. Upon her telling me she had resigned, I took her gentle face in between both my hands, caressing her neck and cheeks ever-so-lightly, remembering in that instant the first time I had kissed her, and told her that I loved her and that everything would be alright. Smiling, a tear welling up and escaping unexpectedly from the corner of her left eye, she whispered back to me, "I'm so proud of you baby", and we kissed, sharing the first and only bit of physical affection we would ever share within the walls of that school.

Now packed up and ready to leave, waiting alone on my department to be called to the office wherein Ralph was required to sign us out, therein giving us our final paychecks, I couldn't help but wonder about the possibility of things having been different, quickly shaking the notion from my mind, angry still at the reality of it all. By twelve ten, the language arts department was called and I hurriedly made my way to the office, not wanting to have to stand around in line, speaking to staff members from my department about my situation. I was the first to arrive and immediately walked straight into Ralph's office. Upon seeing it was me who had entered, he immediately dropped his head slightly and prepared himself for our final conversation.

"Hey Jared", he managed to muster in a noticeably non empathetic voice, to which I replied in an emotionless, yet professionally addressing tone, "Mr. Black", maintaining my integrity and what little self-esteem I retained throughout my numerous ordeals while employed within the district.

"Listen", he began saying, resembling the sound of a father who wrongfully punished his son and was to make him understand that fathers make mistakes too. But abruptly changed his tone of voice, sounding now as if he was indignant and uncaring, saying, "Good luck in the future", and handed me my check, wherein, looking at him for that brief moment, as if time had just stood still, I thought better verbalizing a response. I signed my name to the final paper saying I was officially dismissed for the summer, and for that matter, the rest of my life and as I was about to leave, he extended his hand to me without looking up for me to shake. This was the moment I was to tell him how disappointed I was in not only him but his school as well. The things I'd seen happen working there, cover ups, scandals, corruption, inappropriate behavior, misappropriation of funds. Everything and anything I could think of. But instead, I regained my inner composure and grasped onto my self-control, extended my hand to his, firmly shook it, and sincerely thanked him for the opportunity provided me by both he and his district. It was my last chance to make a lasting impression, telling him what I really thought of not only him but the district in general, when I felt it no longer important. What was important was that I was leaving with my dignity in tact. I could walk out those doors that one last time and hold my head up high, knowing that I did what was required of me, to teach, in the best way I knew how, perpetually maintaining my students' safety and well being at the forefront of my mission. And I had done it!

Once inside my truck, I lowered the window and lit a cigarette, preparing never again to return to the town of Yarseville, much less set foot inside the high school. With the sun at its zenith, I slowly drove out of the parking lot, past the main entrance doors, turning left onto Main Street, wondering about my future.

I would later come to learn that Anthony Vincent Licardello, as was his real full given name, was fired the following year for maintaining an inappropriate sexual relationship with a sixteen year old student but the story never made the papers, the fourth such type of incident in as many years. He called me after the start of the following school year, assuming I knew nothing of his dismissal, acting as if he was seriously considering leaving the job from which he was already terminated. Superintendent Thistle got himself into a bit of trouble, due in part to his having an affair with one of the elementary school teachers in the district, viewing pornography on the internet while in his office, therein violating the technology use agreement that was to be followed by all Yarseville employees, regardless of position, as well as numerous incidents dealing with missing monies and misappropriation of funds, wherein by mid-December, he stepped down, forced to resign. Andrea and her husband filed for divorce on grounds that it was now public knowledge that she was having an affair with the eventual interim Superintendent Ackerman and was constantly turning over employees in the language arts department. And Principal Black was also under investigation by the board for inappropriate practices of which were at the time I learned of this, nonspecific, as well as the astounding turn over rate of employees; fifty-two in the high school alone the year after I left. I also learned that he had become incredibly soured and vindictive; giving bad recommendations to teachers leaving his school, further jeopardizing his own future within the district. Only one of the three vice principals remained from my years in Yarseville, the last actively seeking employment elsewhere.

Thinking back, now a teacher of two years in a completely different school district wherein I now maintain a low profile socially but still teach in a manner the way I see fit, supported by administration as well as my colleagues, I view my experience in Yarseville as a positive one. Sometimes in life we tend to make mistakes and have to reevaluate situations in order to never again have the same things happen. I wouldn't consider working in Yarseville a mistake, but rather a learning experience provided to me wherein I learned more than I ever thought possible. Going in I was an educator, but I came out more educated than I could have ever imagined. And for that, I am truly grateful in regards to my service as not only a teacher of students, but as a student of life as well.